"What kind of barba asked, her voice sha

"A rich one," he said flatl unwise to cross—unless you are prepared to suffer the consequences. But perhaps, *thespinis,* you thought you were immune?"

"How could I possibly have crossed you?" she protested. "Twenty-four hours ago I—I didn't know you existed."

"Whereas I have been aware of you for the past year," he said. "And have looked forward to our meeting. I do not think I shall be disappointed."

The dark eyes went over her. Slowly and quite deliberately stripping her naked, she realized dazedly.

"Please me," he went on. "And you will find me generous."

"And if I don't please you?"

He shrugged. "Then you will learn to do so, and quickly," he returned, almost indifferently. "You have no other option, as I am sure you will come to see when you have considered the matter further."

He paused. "Your clothes and other possessions have already been packed, and tonight you will be flown to Greece where you will wait for me on my island of Pellas."

His slow smile made her shiver.

"I find anticipation increases the appetite—don't you…?"

Harlequin Presents® is pleased to present this new and exciting miniseries!

THE UNTAMED

Arrogant and proud, unashamedly male!

Harlequin Presents® with a retro twist…

Step back in time to when men were men—
and women knew just how to tame them!

Previous titles in this series:

Blackwolf's Redemption
by Sandra Marton

Gray Quinn's Baby
by Susan Stephens

Sara Craven

THE HIGHEST STAKES OF ALL

TORONTO NEW YORK LONDON
AMSTERDAM PARIS SYDNEY HAMBURG
STOCKHOLM ATHENS TOKYO MILAN MADRID
PRAGUE WARSAW BUDAPEST AUCKLAND

ISBN-13: 978-0-373-12992-8

THE HIGHEST STAKES OF ALL

First North American Publication 2011

www.eHarlequin.com

Printed in U.S.A.

THE HIGHEST
STAKES OF ALL

CHAPTER ONE

South of France, 1975

'PICKINGS,' Denys Vernon said with immense satisfaction. 'And very rich pickings by the look of it.'

Stifling a sigh, Joanna put down the *tartine* she was buttering, and followed her father's gaze to the new yacht that had appeared overnight in the bay below the Hotel St Gregoire.

It was certainly large and extremely opulent, effortlessly diminishing the lesser craft anchored nearby. A floating palace, she thought, of gleaming white paint and chrome. Very swish. And suddenly there. Out of nowhere.

'A wealthy sheikh, perhaps.' Denys continued his musings aloud. 'Or even foreign royalty.'

'Or merely someone sheltering from last night's storm,' Joanna suggested more practically. She paused. 'And, speaking of storms, the manager stopped me last night and asked when our bill would be settled. And he wasn't smiling.'

'Infernal bloody cheek,' Denys snorted. 'Gaston Levaux is becoming obsessive about cash. If he's not careful, the whole place will become insufferably bourgeois.'

'Just because he wants to be paid?' Joanna asked mildly. 'I thought making money was our sole reason for being here, too.' She gave him a level look. 'And the fact that we haven't been doing so well lately must have been reported back to the office.'

'I'm still ahead of the game,' Denys said sharply. 'All I need is one good night.' His eyes strayed back to the yacht. 'And one wealthy idiot who thinks he can play poker.'

'And maybe Monsieur Levaux is concerned about his job,' Joanna continued reflectively. 'People are saying openly that the entire BelCote chain is being sold off. He won't want any bad debts on his books when the new owners take over.'

'Well, I'm sure he doesn't need your concern.' Denys looked her over. 'I think you should visit the hotel boutique, my pet. Buy a new dress as a demonstration of good faith.' He nodded. 'Something short and not too sweet to show off your tan.'

'Dad, I have plenty of clothes.' Joanna spoke with a touch of weariness. 'Besides, we have no money to waste on empty gestures.'

'Not waste, darling. Investment. And please keep your voice down when you call me—that,' he added irritably. 'Someone might hear.'

'And draw the correct conclusion that I'm actually your daughter instead of your supposed niece?' She shook her head. 'How long can we keep this farce going?'

And, in particular, how long before you grow up? she wondered in unhappy silence as her father's mouth tightened petulantly. Before you acknowledge that you haven't been forty for some time. That your hair is only blond because it's tinted, and you're not wrinkled because you've had an expensive face-lift.

'It's working very well. For one thing, it explains the same surname on our passports,' Denys retorted. 'And, as I told you at the outset, it doesn't suit my image to have a daughter who's nearly nineteen.'

And it doesn't suit me at all, Joanna thought bitterly. How long will it be before I can have a real life—the life I once planned?

Teaching languages had been her aim. She'd been studying for her A levels prior to university when her mother had been taken suddenly ill, and diagnosed with inoperable cancer. Two months later she was dead, and Joanna's relatively stable existence up to that point ended, too.

Denys, summoned home from America as soon as his wife's condition became known, had been genuinely grief-stricken. It had been his inability to settle rather than any lack of caring that had kept them apart for so much of their married life. Gail Vernon wanted a permanent home for her only child. Denys needed to gamble much as he needed to draw breath.

However, he was a generous if erratic provider, and, to Joanna, he had seemed an almost god-like being, suntanned and handsome, whenever he returned to the UK. A dispenser of laughter and largesse, she thought, his cases stuffed with scent, jewellery and other exotic gifts as well as the elegant clothes he had made for him in the Far East.

'If he ever gets stopped at Customs, he'll end up in jail,' his older brother Martin had muttered.

Yet, somehow, it had never happened. And perhaps Uncle Martin had been right when he also said Denys had the devil's own luck. But lately that luck had not been much in evidence. He'd sustained some heavy losses, and his recoveries had not been as positive as they needed to be.

He was invariably cagey about the exact state of their finances, and Joanna's attempts to discover how they stood had never been successful.

'Everything's fine, my pet,' was his usual airy reply. 'Stop worrying your pretty head and smile.'

A response that had Joanna grinding her teeth. As so much did these days.

At the beginning, of course, it had all seemed like a great adventure. The last thing she'd expected was to be taken out of school and whisked off abroad to share her father's peripatetic lifestyle, travelling from one gambling centre to another as the mood took him.

Uncle Martin and Aunt Sylvie had protested vociferously, saying that she could make a home with them while she finished her education, but Denys had been adamant.

'She's all I have left,' he'd repeated over and over again. 'All that remains of her mother. Can't you understand that I need her with me?' he'd added. 'Besides, a change of scene will be good for her. Get her away from all these painful memories of my lovely Gail.'

With hindsight, Joanna wondered rather sadly if he'd have been so set on her company if she'd still been the quiet, shy child with braces on her teeth. Instead, she'd soared into slender, long-legged womanhood, her chestnut hair falling in a silken swathe to her waist, and green eyes that seemed to ask what the world had to offer.

Which, at first, seemed to be a great deal. The travelling, the hotel suites, the super-charged atmosphere of the casinos had been immensely exciting for an almost eighteen-year-old.

Even the shock when she learned that Denys wasn't prepared to acknowledge their real relationship hadn't detracted too much from the appeal of their nomadic existence. Or not immediately.

She'd realised quite soon that women of all ages found her father attractive, and tried, without much success, not to let it bother her. But while Denys was charming, flattering and grateful, he was determined to make it clear that it would go no further than that.

'I need you to be my shield—keeping my admirers at a distance,' he'd told her seriously. His tone had become wheedling. 'Treat it as part of the game, darling. Mummy always told me how good you were in your school plays. Now's your chance to show me how well you can really act.'

But why were you never there to see for yourself? Joanna wanted to ask, but didn't, because her father was continuing.

'All you have to do, my pet, is stick close to me, smile and say as little as possible.'

On the whole, Joanna thought she'd managed pretty well, even when the leering looks and muttered remarks from many of the men she encountered made her want to run away and hide.

The mother of Jackie, her best friend at school, had become involved in the women's movement, and held consciousness-raising sessions at her house. The iniquity of women being regarded as sex objects by men, had been among the favourite themes at those meetings, and while she and Jackie had giggled about it afterwards, Joanna now thought ruefully that Mrs Henderson might have had a point.

Eventually, it had all ceased to be a game, and she'd begun to see her new life for the tawdry sham it really was, and be troubled by it. Realising at the same time that there was no feasible way out. That, for the time being, she was trapped.

Denys was speaking again, his voice excited. 'I'm going to start making enquiries. Find out who the new arrival is, and if he's likely to visit the Casino.' He gave her a minatory nod. 'I'll see you back here after lunch.'

Here we go again, Joanna thought with a sigh as she heard the suite door close behind him. Looking for a non-existent pot of gold at the end of a dodgy rainbow.

'All I need is one big win.' She had lost count of how many times her father had said this over the past months.

And she sent up a silent prayer to the god of gamblers that the unknown owner would stay safely aboard his yacht for the duration. Although that, of course, would not help with the looming threat of the hotel bill.

She stayed on the balcony for a while, drinking another cup of coffee and enjoying the sunlit freshness of the morning after the unexpected heavy rain with thunder, lightning and squally winds of the previous night. But she was still unable to fully relax, not while the question of how long they could go on living like this continued to haunt her.

'You're my little mascot,' Denys had told her jubilantly in the early days, but she hadn't brought him much luck recently.

I shall have to start avoiding the front desk and use the staff entrance in the daytime, too, instead of just the evenings, she thought wryly as she pushed back her chair and went through the sliding glass doors into the sitting room.

The chambermaids were due soon, and she had to make sure that all signs of her nightly occupation of the sofa were removed from their eagle-eyed scrutiny.

It seemed a long time since their budget had been able to run to a suite with two bedrooms, and while she didn't begrudge her father his comfortable night's sleep, quite understanding that he needed to wake completely refreshed in order to keep his wits sharp, nevertheless she missed the peace and privacy which the sitting room could not provide.

When she was sure all was as it should be, she packed sun oil, her coin purse and a paperback book into her raffia bag, together with two leftover rolls from breakfast wrapped in tissues to provide her with a makeshift lunch.

She pinned her hair up into a loose knot, covering it with a wide-brimmed straw hat, then pulled a white cheesecloth tunic over her turquoise bikini, donned her sunglasses and picked up her towel. Thus camouflaged, she set off down to the swimming pool.

Few people, if any, recognised her in the daytime. Wearing espadrilles instead of the platform-soled high heels that Denys insisted on took at least a couple of inches from her height, and with her hair hidden, her face scrubbed clean of its evening make-up, and wearing a modestly cut bikini, she attracted little attention even from men who'd been sending her openly amorous looks the night before.

The St Gregoire charged a hefty number of francs for the hire of its loungers on the paved sun terraces, so Joanna invariably chose instead to spread her towel on one of the lawns encircling the pool, a practice not forbidden, but muttered at by the man who came to collect the money from the paying guests.

Ignore him, Joanna told herself, rubbing oil into her exposed skin already tanned a judicious golden brown. And try to pretend the grass isn't damp while you're about it.

She turned on to her stomach, and retrieved the book she'd found in a second-hand store just before they'd left for France, a former prize-winning detective story by a British author called P. D. James, which had attracted Joanna because its title, *An Unsuitable Job for a Woman,* seemed to sum up her current situation.

Maybe I could become a private investigator, she mused, finding her place in the story. Except I don't have someone likely to die and leave me a detective agency.

A more likely scenario, if things went badly wrong this time, was a swift return to the UK and a job for Denys in Uncle Martin's light engineering works. It had been offered before, prompted, Joanna suspected, by her uncle's very real concern for her future. Although he'd had plenty of troubles of his own in the past few years with the imposition of the three-day week, strikes and constant power cuts to contend with.

But her father had replied, as always, that it would kill him to be tied to a desk, and he had to be a free spirit, although Joanna could see no freedom in having bills you were unable to pay. One day, she thought, he might have to bite on the bullet and accept Uncle Martin's offer.

And for me, a secretarial course, I suppose, she mused resignedly. But I'd settle for that, if it meant a normal life. And not being lonely any more. I'm just not the adventurous type, and I only wish I'd realised that much sooner.

It wasn't really possible to make friends when they were so often on the move, but other girls tended to steer clear anyway. And apart from one occasion in Australia, which she'd tried hard to forget, she'd been left severely alone by young men, too.

She stopped herself on the point of another sigh. Forget the self-pity, she adjured herself, and find out how private investigator Cordelia Gray is going to solve her first solo case.

At that moment, she heard her name called, and turned to see Julie Phillips approaching across the grass.

Joanna sat up smiling. 'Hi, there.' She looked around. 'What have you done with Matthew?'

'Chris has taken him down to the village.' Julie sat down beside her, shading her eyes from the sun. 'He wanted to buy something for his mother from that little pottery shop.' She sighed. 'I can hardly believe our week is up. And, would you believe, we're almost sorry to be going home. For which we have you to thank, of course.'

'That's nonsense,' Joanna said roundly. 'It was just lucky I happened to be at the desk that day, and was able to help.'

She'd been waiting to buy some stamps when she'd over-heard the clearly distressed young couple protesting to an unsympathetic desk clerk about the hotel's policy of barring babies and young children from the restaurant after seven p.m.

As their French was clearly minimal, she'd helped trans-late for them, even though their objections were ultimately met with a shrug of complete indifference.

They'd adjourned to the terrace bar for coffee, where Joanna had learned they'd won their South of France holiday in a mag-azine competition, but their intended destination had been a three-star hotel in the BelCote chain.

A fire had resulted in a grudging upgrade to the St Gregoire.

'But we felt from the moment we got here yesterday that they didn't really want us.' Julie had said. 'They made a fuss about putting a cot in the bungalow, told us there was no babysitting service, then dropped the bombshell about the restaurant. If we wanted to eat there, we had to have the special children's supper at six.'

She'd sighed. 'We're just so disappointed with it all. It isn't a bit as we'd hoped. Now we feel we simply want to go home.'

Joanna could only sympathise but she was unsurprised. The hotel was a place where little children might be seen but not heard, and Matt had a good pair of lungs on him.

But the St Gregoire had accepted this family, however

reluctantly, and it was totally unfair to prevent them sampling the culinary delights on offer in the restaurant.

She took a deep breath. 'I've had an idea,' she said. 'We—I—never have dinner until at least nine. If you're prepared to eat early, I'll come to the bungalow each night as soon as the children's supper is over and look after Matt for you, so that you can dine together in the restaurant.'

There was a silence, then Julie said, 'No, we couldn't ask you. Couldn't impose like that.'

'I'd love to do it.' Joanna bent, and ran a finger down Matt's round pink cheek, receiving a toothless grin as a reward. 'I can't produce any references,' she added ruefully. 'But I used to babysit a lot for our neighbours in England. And I—I miss it.'

Husband and wife exchanged glances, then Chris leaned forward, his pleasant, freckled face serious.

'Well, if you really mean it, we'd be endlessly grateful. We were actually going to find out today how much it would cost to cut our losses and fly home.'

'Oh, you can't do that.' Joanna shook her head decisively. 'Because the food really is fantastic. You mustn't miss out on it.'

The final details of the arrangement were hammered out there and then. Julie assured her that Matt was a good sleeper who rarely woke in the evenings, but that she'd leave a bottle ready just in case. In return Joanna made it clear she would accept no payment whatsoever.

And on that they'd shaken hands on the deal.

Denys had received the news with far less amiability.

'What the hell are you thinking of?' he demanded incredulously. 'Who are these people?'

'A sweet couple with a nice baby they can't take into the restaurant for dinner,' Joanna informed him calmly.

'Then why don't they order room service, or switch from dinner to lunch?' he demanded irritably.

Joanna gave him a straight look. 'Because they'd be charged

a lot extra and they can't afford it. Not a pleasant position to be in,' she added with faint emphasis. 'And as long as I'm ready to eat with you later, why should you care?'

'Because you might be seen, and there could be talk. You're not here as some kind of domestic help, Joanna,' he added with a snap.

'No,' she said. 'But strangely I find I prefer it. And, whatever you say, I've promised. They're nice people, very different to those I usually have to mix with these days, and I have no intention of letting them down.'

It was a decision she hadn't regretted once, not even on the rare occasions when Matt had woken and grizzled. That brief hour or so in the lamp-lit peace of the bungalow's small terrace had become a welcome refuge.

A blissful break before she had to be on show, pretending to be someone else, she thought now with an inward sigh.

She said, 'I shall really miss my baby-watch.'

'Like an aching tooth,' Julie laughed. 'But surely you'll be leaving soon yourself, won't you?'

Joanna looked away. 'I—I'm not certain. It's not really up to me.'

'Well, think about us slaving away in the UK while you're still living in the lap of luxury.'

Joanna's smile held a touch of bitterness. 'There's more than one form of slavery,' she said quietly. 'And, believe me, I'd be out of here tomorrow, given the chance.'

Julie stared at her, her bright face suddenly troubled. 'Are you really so unhappy?' she asked gently.

'No, no, of course not.' Joanna shook her head. 'Just a touch of the blues, that's all. I—I have some big career choices looming.' *And that's only part of it.*

Julie got to her feet. 'Well, if you want my opinion, you should become a nanny,' she said, adding hastily, 'But not the stiff and starchy sort. I think you'd be magic, and then, when Chris and I get seriously rich, we can hire you.'

'I'll bear it in mind,' Joanna said with forced cheerfulness.

'And as for wanting to get out of here,' Julie went on, 'my gran always says, "Be careful what you wish for, because you might get it." So watch yourself, and please don't get whisked away before dinner tonight.'

Joanna laughed. 'I promise. But after dinner—all bets are off.'

Alone again, she returned to her book but found it difficult to concentrate. Julie's suggestion that she might become a professional nanny had set new ideas and career possibilities buzzing in her head, and she couldn't dismiss them, although she could foresee the problems of trying to free herself from the current situation.

She knew that Uncle Martin would get her back to the UK if she asked for his help.

But Dad needs me, she thought. He said so from the start. Things were going well for him then. So how can I desert him when the going's got tough?

She collected her things together, put on her tunic, and began to stroll back towards the hotel. She hadn't gone far when she spotted the hotel manager heading towards her, looking harassed and talking volubly, hands waving, to a plump middle-aged man with a swarthy skin and heavy moustache who was walking beside him, expensively dressed in a silk suit.

And Monsieur Levaux is the last person I need to run into right now, Joanna thought grimly. Plus I wouldn't fool him even if I was wearing a sack over my head.

She turned swiftly away, taking a narrower path to the right which circled the gardens and led out onto a small promontory beyond.

As usual, she had it to herself. Few of the guests ventured far from the pool, the beach or the various bars.

She lifted her face to meet the slight breeze from the sea as she walked across the tussocks of grass to the farthest point, and looked out over the rippling azure water.

The big yacht was still there, riding at anchor like a dignified swan, with small boats circling it like inquisitive ducklings.

On impulse, Joanna went over to the telescope that some-one had helpfully erected on a small concrete platform, and fed the requisite number of centimes into the slot. She adjusted the focus and guided the tube into a slow sweep of the whole bay before returning to its current most prominent feature.

The first thing she looked for was the name, but the letters along the bow were in Greek, so she was none the wiser.

However, it couldn't belong to Onassis, because he'd died the previous year, nor, indeed, the rich sheikh her father had been hoping for.

And is that a good thing or a bad? Joanna wondered wryly.

In close-up, the yacht was even more spectacular, and Joanna found herself speculating how many crew members it took to preserve that stringently immaculate appearance. There certainly didn't seem to be many of them around at the moment, scrubbing and polishing.

In fact, she could see just one solitary individual leaning on the rail of the upper deck, and adjusted the telescope for a closer look. Her immediate thought was that he didn't belong in his pristine surroundings. On the contrary.

He wore no shirt, and she was treated to an uninterrupted view of deeply bronzed powerful shoulders and a muscular torso. With his tousled mane of black hair and the shadow of a beard masking his chin, he looked more like a pirate than a deckhand. In fact he made the place look distinctly untidy, she thought, deciding that he was probably someone from the engine room who'd come up for a breath of air.

She saw his hand move, and something glint in the sunshine. And with a sharp, startled catch of her breath, she suddenly realised that the tables had been turned.

That she herself was now under scrutiny—through a powerful pair of binoculars. And that he was grinning at her, displaying very white teeth, and lifting his hand in a casual, almost mocking salute.

How had he known she was looking at him? she asked herself as a wave of embarrassed heat swamped her from head to toe. And why on earth had she allowed herself to be caught in the act like some—some peeping Thomasina.

On the other hand, why wasn't he swabbing the decks or splicing the mainbrace—whatever that was? Doing something useful instead of—spying back?

Feeling intensely stupid, and wanting to scream in vexation at the same time, Joanna hurriedly abandoned the telescope and walked away with as much dignity as she could muster.

Which wasn't easy when every instinct she possessed and every nerve-ending in her body was telling her with total certainty that he was watching her go.

And knowing at the same time that it would be quite fatal to look back and check—even for a moment.

CHAPTER TWO

'So THERE you are.' Denys marched briskly into the sitting room, kicking the door shut behind him.

Joanna, curled up in the corner of the sofa, finishing off the remains of her breakfast rolls which had not improved with keeping, glanced up warily.

'It's where you told me to be,' she pointed out mildly, observing with faint disquiet the brightness in his eyes, and the tinge of excited red in his face. There was a bunched tension about him too that she remembered from other times. That, and the way he kept clenching and opening one fist.

She added, 'Has something happened?'

'It has indeed, my pet. We're about to hit the jackpot—big-time.' He paused for effect. 'Do you know the name of that yacht in the bay?'

Oh, God, she thought, cringing inwardly as she remembered that insolent, mocking grin. It would have to be that.

'I didn't learn Greek at school,' she said. 'Only Latin.'

He waved an impatient hand. 'Well, she's called *Persephone*. And she's owned by no less a person than Vassos Gordanis.'

Joanna frowned. 'Should I have heard of him?'

'You're hearing now.' Denys came to sit beside her. 'He's Atlas Airlines.' He counted on his fingers. 'He's the Andromeda tanker fleet. He's the Hellenica hotel chain—the outfit currently buying the building we're living in, along with all the other BelCote hotels.'

He smiled exultantly. 'He's one of the super-rich. Had the wit to stay out of harm's way on his boat and some island he owns in the Aegean, avoiding politics during these past years in Greece when the Colonels were in charge. But when the Junta was finally overthrown last year he began to operate freely again, and they say he's set to climb into the financial stratosphere.'

Joanna suddenly remembered the portly man in the silk suit she'd seen with Gaston Levaux. So that was what a Greek tycoon looked like, she thought, reflecting that the heavy-jowled face had possessed undoubted shrewdness if nothing else to write home about.

'How did you discover all this?' she asked.

'Nora Van Dyne told me over bridge this morning.' His face clouded momentarily. 'She'll never make a card player. Talks too damned much. But she knows everything that's going on, and this time she told me something I wanted to hear.'

And don't I wish she hadn't? Joanna thought wanly. Why couldn't she go on chatting about the New York cultural scene, the cute things her grandchildren said last Thanksgiving, and what her late husband paid for all that wonderful jewellery she wears morning, noon and night?

Denys leaned forward. 'Do you know why he decided to buy the St Gregoire? Because he comes here each year to play poker with some of his cronies and business connections and has got to like the place. They have dinner in a private suite on the top floor, then they get down to the real business of the evening—by invitation only, of course.'

'I see.' Joanna managed to conceal her relief. 'Well, that settles that.'

'On the contrary, my pet. I had a quiet word with Levaux, asked him to pull a few strings. Get me into the game.' He smiled with satisfaction. 'And somehow he's done it. Probably thinks it's the only way he'll get paid.'

Joanna moved restively. 'Dad—are you quite sure about this?'

'Have a little faith, darling.' Denys spoke reproachfully. 'It's the answer to our prayers.'

Not for me, Joanna thought. Not for me.

'But I'll need you to pull all the stops out tonight,' he added, confirming her worst fears. 'So get down to the boutique. I've already spoken to Marie Claude, and she's picked out a dress for you.'

'But it's a private game,' Joanna protested desperately. 'You—you said so. I wouldn't be allowed in.'

'That's fixed, too. Levaux has explained I can't play without you—my talisman—my little lucky charm—and it appears that Mr Gordanis is prepared to stretch a point on this occasion.'

He paused. 'According to Nora, he's a widower with more than just an eye for the girls. In fact he's got one hell of a reputation. So you definitely have to be there.'

Joanna recoiled inwardly, knowing only too well what would be expected of her tonight and with a man whose sole attraction had to be his money. Because it would never be his looks.

She thought how she would have to smile and flutter her mascaraed lashes. Would have to toss back her hair and cross her legs as she perched artlessly on the arm of Denys's chair, distracting his opponent for that vital instant when he most needed to concentrate on the cards in his hand.

After all, she'd done it so often before, she thought bitterly. Had learned to move her young, slim body in deliberate, provocative enticement in order to make men stare at her, their fantasies going into overdrive, and their minds dangerously off the game.

She'd hoped, after the incident in Australia the previous year, that she'd be let off the hook, but her reprieve had only lasted a couple of months. Then it was business as usual, responding, when Denys signalled by brushing his forefinger across his lips, as if she was on auto-pilot.

She felt a knot of tension tighten in her chest. 'Dad—I'd really rather not be involved in this.'

'But you already are, my pet.' There was a harsh note in his voice. 'If we can't pay our hotel bill, you won't be spared. You know that. So be a good girl and collect your dress from Marie Claude. And I don't want you rushing to get ready this evening,' he added warningly. 'You need to take your time. Make sure you look dazzling. So tell those people they'll have to look after their own brat for once.'

Joanna sat up very straight. 'No,' she said. 'I can't. I won't. Or you'll be on your own in that suite tonight, looking down the barrel of this tycoon's gun.'

'You'll do as you're told, young lady—'

'No, Dad,' she interrupted quietly and firmly. 'Not this time. After all, you can hardly drag me in there by force, not if I'm to convince this Mr Gordanis that he's everything I've ever wanted in a man.'

She took a deep breath. 'But first I'm going to babysit for Chris and Julie, or the deal's off. And I have to tell you that this is going to be the last time I act as a diversion for you, because each time I do it I feel sick to my stomach.'

She paused again. 'You told me you wanted me with you because I was all you had left. Because I reminded you of my mother. So what do you think she'd say if she could see me— paraded around like this, like some—cheap tart?'

'My dear child.' Denys's tone was uneasy as well as placatory. 'I think you're taking our little deception much too seriously.'

'Am I?' Joanna asked bitterly. 'I wonder if the men whose wallets I've helped to empty would agree with you.'

'Well, you certainly don't have to worry about Mr Gordanis,' Denys said with faint surliness. 'His bank account will survive a quick raid.'

'I'm not worried about him,' she said quietly. 'It's you.' She hesitated. 'Dad—swear to me that if you start winning tonight you'll get out while you're ahead. Make enough to cover our expenses here and a couple of plane tickets to somewhere else, then stop.' She put a hand on his arm. 'Please—I'm begging you. Because I need a real life.'

He sighed impatiently. 'Oh, all right. If that's what you want. But I think you're being quite ridiculous, Joanna.'

'I can deal with that,' she said. 'It's feeling dirty that I can't handle.' She paused again, awkwardly. 'There won't be any other—problems, will there?'

His mouth tightened. 'That was a one-off,' he said. 'As I told you at the time.'

Yes, she thought unhappily. You told me. So I have to trust you. And I just pray that when tonight's over I'll feel able to do that again.

The dress from the boutique did nothing to reassure her, or lift the bleakness of her mood. It was a black crochet affair, with a deeply scooped neck and a skirt that just reached mid-thigh. The sleeves provided the most concealment, fitting closely to the elbow then flaring to the wrist, but that was little comfort when, underneath, the dress accommodated nothing more than a body stocking, giving the troubling impression that she could be naked.

She'd looked at herself in the mirror of the tiny changing room with something like despair. 'Surely there must be something else? Something not quite so—revealing?'

Marie Claude had shrugged, her eyes cynical. 'You have a good body. Use it while you are young.'

So Joanna took the dress back to the suite, and hung it in the *armoire*.

She spent the rest of the afternoon washing her hair and conditioning it until it shone with all the rich depth of a horse chestnut, then gave herself a pedicure, painting her toenails in the clear light red that matched her fingertips.

Lastly, she arranged the cosmetics she planned to use later on the dressing table, together with her precious bottle of Miss Dior, before changing into shorts and a tee shirt, and heading off to Chris and Julie's bungalow situated on the farthest edge of the hotel gardens.

Its remoteness didn't bother Joanna, who loved the sense of privacy imparted by the surrounding hedges of flowering shrubs.

'I expect we've been dumped here out of the way,' Julie had confided. 'But that's fine by us. Because if Matt decides to squall we don't have to worry about disturbing the neighbours.'

It had another advantage, too, thought Joanna. There was no direct sea view, so she was spared the sight of the *Persephone* together with her owner and any stray members of her crew who might still be hanging around, behaving like God's gift to women.

The sun was getting lower in the sky, but it was still warm, so she let herself in and took a bottle of chilled Coke from the refrigerator in the tiny kitchen, and the copy of *Watership Down* which Julie had promised to leave for her 'together with a box of tissues. It's all about rabbits'.

'And I'll give you *Jaws,*' Chris had teased. 'By way of contrast.'

She settled herself with a sigh into one of the cane chairs on the small verandah, relishing the peace, longing to start her new book, but unable to dismiss from her mind the horrors she knew were awaiting her later that night.

She had watched poker games in the past until her eyes glazed over, as they often did when a game continued through the small hours into dawn. But that was through boredom as much as tiredness. She had tried at first to establish some kind of interest in the game, but she still didn't follow its intricacies or understand its attraction.

In fact I wouldn't care, she told herself, if I never saw another pack of cards as long as I live.

But she wasn't likely to be bored this evening. Far too much depended on it, and the role of mindless dolly-bird would be even more difficult to sustain than usual.

It was a good ten minutes before Chris and Julie arrived with the baby, looking harassed.

'He's been really grumpy at supper,' Julie reported. 'Started crying and threw his food on the floor. I could feel waves of disapproval reaching me from the nannies all over the room.'

She unstrapped a red-faced Matt from his pushchair and lifted him out, whereupon he began to cry again, a steady, bad-tempered wail.

'Leave him to me,' said Joanna, sounding more reassuring than she actually felt. 'Go and have a smashing meal together, and I'll bath him and get him settled.'

Julie looked at her with a mixture of doubt and relief. 'Well, if you're quite sure…'

Half an hour later, Joanna wasn't certain of very much at all. Matt was standing up in his cot, roaring with discontent and shaking the bars, only desisting when Joanna picked him up and held him.

'You haven't got a temperature,' she told him. 'And I don't think you've got a pain anywhere. I suspect, my lad, you're just having a major strop.'

Any attempt to get him back in the cot, however, met with stern resistance, so in the end Joanna bowed to the inevitable, heated up his milk, and carried him out to the twilit verandah, settling his squirming red-faced person gently but firmly in the crook of her arm.

'This had better not become a habit,' she said, dropping a kiss on his silky head.

By the time he'd drunk nearly all the milk his eyelids were drooping, but he was still attempting to cry intermittently as he fought against sleep.

'Drastic measures called for, I think,' Joanna whispered to herself, and, cuddling him close, she began to sing, clearly and very sweetly, a song from her own early childhood, '"There were ten green bottles, hanging on the wall…"'

As the number of bottles gradually decreased, she allowed

her voice to sink lower and lower, until it was barely a murmur, and Matt, thumb in mouth, was finally fast asleep.

Joanna sat for a while, looking down, smiling, at the sleeping baby. A faint breeze had risen, bringing a delicious waft of the garden's evening scents. And also, she realised, something more alien. A faint but unmistakable aroma of cigar smoke.

But Chris, she thought, puzzled, was a non-smoker. Besides, it would be another half-hour or more before he and Julie returned.

Suddenly nervous, she wanted to call *Who's there?* but hesitated for fear of waking Matt. In the next instant she thought she could hear the sound of footsteps quietly receding, yet wasn't entirely sure.

She got carefully to her feet, listening hard, but there was nothing—only the distant sound of the sea.

I'm imagining things, she thought. Because I'm feeling jumpy about tonight. That's all it is.

Which was probably why the breeze seemed suddenly colder, too, she thought, shivering as she carried Matt inside and closed the door.

The crochet dress did not improve on acquaintance, Joanna thought, sighing, as she made a last check of her appearance. Worn with knee-length white boots that laced up the front, the outfit presented itself as the kind of sexy tease which needed a certain amount of sophistication to carry off, and she knew she was nowhere near that level.

However, she'd done her best. She'd used the heavier foundation she reserved for these occasions, transforming her face into a blank canvas, then smoothed shimmering silver on to her eyelids, accentuating it with softly smudged black liner, before adding two coats of mascara to her long lashes. The bronze blusher on her cheekbones had a touch of glitter, too, and she had applied a deeper shade of the same colour to her mouth.

Fancy dress and a mask, she told herself, as she applied

scent to her pulses, her temples, and the valley between her breasts. Think of it that way.

There was room for very little but the basics in her tiny evening purse, and as she searched in her shoulder bag for the compact of pressed translucent powder she always wore, she found the slip of paper Chris and Julie had given her, with their name, address and telephone number.

It was the nearest to a friendship she'd achieved since leaving Britain, and it was also a possible lifeline, she thought wryly as she tucked it carefully into her wallet.

Denys was pacing the sitting room, and he gave a nod of judicious satisfaction as she emerged from the bedroom.

'Once dinner is over,' he told her, 'someone will come to escort us up to the Gordanis suite.'

'Very formal.' Her tone was dry. 'As are you,' she added, removing a speck of fluff from the lapel of his dinner jacket. 'Is the black tie strictly necessary?'

He shrugged. 'It's a big night. And a very big game. Mr Gordanis can afford to impose his own rules.'

But can you afford to play by them? was the question she did not dare ask as they took the lift down to the dining room.

She ate sparingly at dinner, and drank even less, noting that her father was being equally abstemious. Afterwards they drank coffee on the terrace outside the dining room while the time ticked slowly past, building the tension inside her.

She said, 'Do you think it's not going to happen—that we've been forgotten?'

'No.' Denys shook his head. 'Apparently, he plays for amusement first with some of his friends. After they leave, the stakes rise and the game becomes serious. We'll be sent for soon.'

But it was well after midnight when Gaston Levaux appeared unsmilingly beside them. 'Monsieur Vernon. I am here on behalf of Monsieur Vassos Gordanis who invites you to join him.' He paused. 'I should warn you that you will be required to pay one thousand dollars simply to buy into the game.'

Oh, God, Joanna thought, suddenly weak with relief. We

haven't got a thousand cents. I never thought I'd be glad to be broke.

But her father was meeting Monsieur Levaux's questioning glance with an airy shrug. 'There's no problem about that. I was told he played in dollars and I have the money.'

Thanks, no doubt, to Mrs Van Dyne, Joanna whispered under her breath, silently cursing all rich American widows.

'I must also caution you that Monsieur Gordanis is a formidable opponent. It is not too late for you to make your excuses—or at least those of the *mademoiselle*,' he added.

'You really mustn't concern yourself.' There was a note of steel in Denys's voice. 'I'm looking forward to the game, and so is Joanna—aren't you, darling?'

Joanna saw the manager's mouth tighten. As they walked to the lift, he spoke to her quietly in French. 'Do you ever suffer from migraine, *mademoiselle?* If so, I suggest you develop one very quickly.'

If only, thought Joanna, aware that she was being warned and a little startled by it. Knowing, too, that she would probably have to develop a brain tumour in order to deflect Denys from his purpose.

When they reached the top floor, a small group of men were waiting in the corridor, laughing and talking. As Joanna emerged they fell silent, and she saw glances being exchanged, and even heard a murmur of, *'Oh, là là!'* from one of them.

You take no notice, she reminded herself stonily. You behave as if you were a dummy in a shop window. You don't see, hear, talk or think. And you just pray that Dad wins—and wins quickly.

The double doors at the end of the corridor swung open as they approached. The room ahead was hazy with tobacco smoke, and the smell of alcohol hung in the air. Half a dozen men were standing around, chatting as they waited for play to recommence, while a waiter in a white jacket was moving among them, refilling glasses and emptying ashtrays.

So many other rooms, she thought. So many other times, yet all the same.

Except, she realised, that tonight there were no other women present. It was then she saw Vassos Gordanis walking towards the door, smiling expansively and talking to a man in a dark blue tuxedo, who also seemed to be leaving.

As he saw Joanna, the smile faded from his pouched face, and she felt herself quail inwardly beneath his hard, opaque gaze.

A sudden hush had fallen on the room as everyone turned to look at her, too, and she knew an overwhelming impulse to turn and run, only Denys's hand was under her arm, urging her forward.

'Come along, my sweet,' he said. 'Come and meet our host.'

She thought, But we've just walked past him… And then the group in front of her fell back, revealing a circular table littered with chips and a scatter of playing cards.

But, more importantly, revealing also the man who was seated facing her across the green baize.

She knew him at once, of course. He was clean-shaven now, and the curling black hair was combed back, but the arrogant lines of his face with its high-bridged nose and strongly marked chin were quite unmistakable, as were the heavy-lidded dark eyes and that hard, frankly sensual mouth that she'd last seen smiling at her from the deck of *Persephone*.

Only he wasn't smiling now, and the hooded eyes studied her without any particular expression in their obsidian depths as he lounged back in his chair, his tie hanging loose and his frilled white shirt half-unbuttoned, providing her with an unwilling reminder of the bronze muscularity she'd seen only that morning.

He had a half-smoked cheroot in one hand, while the other held a short string of amber beads, which he was sliding constantly and restlessly through his long fingers.

He did not get to his feet at her approach, and instinct told her this was not prompted by any acceptance of male and female equality as preached by Jackie's mother, who saw any demonstration of masculine courtesy as a form of subjugation and therefore an implied insult.

No, this insult was quite intentional, she thought, designed to show her exactly where she stood in his personal scheme of things—which seemed to hover somewhere between contempt and indifference.

Why didn't you just bar me? she wanted to ask him. Tell my father that women were taboo? God knows I'd have been so grateful.

Instead, here she was, a total fish out of water, the cynosure of all eyes.

'Oh, Dad,' she whispered to herself, swallowing as Gaston Levaux began to perform the introductions. 'You really miscalculated here.'

However, on the plus side, Vassos Gordanis could not possibly recognise her. After all, she looked totally different from the girl in the straw hat whom he'd seen earlier that day. Her distinctive hair had been completely hidden then, while the heavy layer of make-up she was now wearing completed her disguise.

'And now,' Monsieur Levaux added with open reluctance, 'may I present to you Mademoiselle Joanna.'

'Ah, yes, I was informed she would be joining us.' His voice was low-pitched and husky, his English good in spite of his marked accent. The dark eyes swept her from head to foot in a glance that both assessed and dismissed. The firm mouth curled with faint insolence. 'So this is Kyrios Vernon's—lucky charm.'

She heard smothered laughter from the group behind her, and felt her skin warm.

'If she remains silent, then she may stay,' Vassos Gordanis went on. 'Tell me, *kyrie,* is she that miracle—a woman who knows her place and can keep her mouth shut? Or would it be better to send her back to her room before we begin?'

'Yes,' Joanna pleaded under breath. 'Oh, please—*yes.*'

But Denys was managing to mask his obvious discomfiture with a smile. 'She's indeed my mascot, Mr Gordanis. If she goes, she may take my luck with her. And she knows how to behave at these little gatherings. You have my word for it.'

'Yes,' Vassos Gordanis said softly, drawing on his cheroot and regarding its glowing end almost dispassionately. 'I am sure I can believe that.' He added silkily, 'And we should all enjoy such good fortune.'

Slipping the beads into the pocket of his dinner jacket, he gestured abruptly for a chair to be brought for Joanna and stationed exactly opposite to where he himself was sitting.

Which was the last thing she'd expected—or wanted, she thought, forcing a taut smile as she moved to the offered seat. Usually she kept her distance at the edge of the room until Denys made an excuse to summon her to his side. As she sat down, she tried unobtrusively to smooth her brief skirt over her thighs, and realised that Vassos Gordanis was watching the nervous movement, the corner of his mouth curling sardonically.

Remember what you told yourself earlier, she thought, taking a deep breath, and folding her hands carefully in her lap. You don't talk, you don't hear, you don't think. And now—above all—you don't look back at *him.*

'Gentlemen.' Their host acknowledged his other guests with a faint inclination of the head. 'Join me, if you please.'

He signalled again, and one of the dealers from the Casino came forward, gathering up the cards from the previous session before removing the cellophane cover from an unopened deck and beginning to shuffle it, swiftly and expertly. He dealt out six cards face upwards to decide the seating, and to her relief Denys was allotted the place beside her, with a tall blond American called Chuck on the other side.

Fresh decanters of whisky and brandy were placed on a side table, while around the table jackets were discarded and cigarettes and cigars were lit.

The stage is set, Joanna thought, and the serious business of the evening is about to commence.

And knew she had never felt so uneasy in her life.

CHAPTER THREE

THE game began quietly enough, the betting conservative, no very startling hands, and the atmosphere round the table relaxed.

Providing that I discount my own state of mind, Joanna thought wryly, trying to draw comfort from the air of calm confidence that her father was currently exuding. But it was still early in the proceedings, she knew, and the players would simply be testing each other's strengths and weaknesses.

At the same time, she was conscious that the pair of them were very much outsiders. That the rest—a couple of Frenchmen, a burly South African and her American neighbour—were all clearly long-standing friends and acquaintances of Vassos Gordanis, and each of them powerful and successful in his own right. Not the kind of company expected to welcome strangers into their exclusive and wealthy midst.

So, she wondered, what are we doing here? Why was it allowed?

The person who might have known, of course, was Gaston Levaux, but he'd left while the first hand was being dealt. He wasn't a friend by any stretch of the imagination, but for a moment she'd sensed he could be a reluctant ally.

And at least he'd never been openly hostile like the man she'd originally mistaken for Vassos Gordanis, who'd turned out to be one of several solidly built employees, stationed a deferential couple of feet behind their boss's chair.

Joanna was well aware that this man's overtly inimical gaze was focussed on her, and had been since the game began, and wondered if Denys had also noticed. And if so, would he take warning?

His decision to bring her tonight had been a big mistake, she thought, biting her lip, so the best she could do was keep still and try to be as unobtrusive as possible, keeping her eyes fixed on her clasped hands and registering no reaction to the run of play.

And her conviction that she was surplus to requirements was soon confirmed, when, after the first hour's play, Denys was winning quite comfortably without any dubious assistance from her.

It was true that the pots were only moderate, but that couldn't be allowed to matter. Not when they were building steadily towards their agreed purpose.

Just keep going in the same way, Daddy, please, she appealed silently, and we can be out of this room, this hotel, this place and on our way elsewhere by noon tomorrow.

At the same time, she couldn't avoid an odd feeling that the play so far had been almost deliberately restrained.

'Cigarette, honey?' The usual break had been called in the proceedings, and Chuck was offering her his pack of Chesterfields.

'No, thank you.' The room already felt like an oven, and her eyes were stinging from the smoke. She noticed thankfully that a member of the Gordanis entourage, in response to a murmured instruction, was sliding open one of the heavy glass doors which led out on to the balcony.

'Then how about a Scotch or some bourbon?' Her neighbour signalled to the waiter.

She shook her head. 'I—I don't drink spirits.'

'You don't smoke or drink? Then your vices must be the more interesting kind,' he drawled.

Think what you like, Joanna advised him silently. And then go to hell.

As the waiter came to her side she asked for Perrier water, and noticed his swift enquiring glance at Vassos Gordanis and saw the swift, barely perceptible nod in reply.

He's in control of everything, she thought with a sudden shiver. The air we breathe. Even what we have to drink.

She found herself suddenly wondering how old he was. He looked to be only in his early to mid-thirties, yet in spite of that he'd managed somehow to survive the dangers of the past few years in Greece under the Colonels, and prosper.

She recalled that Denys had mentioned he was a widower, and wondered how long he'd been married, and when his wife had died. Then paused, startled.

Now, why would I want to know that? she asked herself blankly. When there are other aspects of the situation that should concern me more?

Under the general buzz of conversation, she turned to Denys. She said very quietly, 'I'm being watched.'

'Of course you are, my pet.' He flashed a conspiratorial smile at her. 'You're a very beautiful girl, and I want you to be looked at.'

'But it's not in the right way or by the right person,' she protested, troubled. 'I really think it would be better if I found some reason to leave.'

'Don't be silly, darling.' His smile widened, became fixed. 'Everything's fine and I need you to stay exactly where you are. They're raising the ante and the stakes are about to become very interesting.' He took a satisfied breath. 'We're on our way, sweetheart. Trust me.'

'Then at least allow me to get some fresh air before you make our fortune.' She rose restlessly from her chair and walked towards the balcony door, taking care to look at no one, and to ignore the inevitable glances that came her way.

Once outside, she stood for a moment filling her lungs with a couple of deep, steadying breaths before advancing to the elaborate metal railing and leaning against it, moving her shoulders gently in an attempt to ease the tension in her muscles.

The darkness seemed to wrap her like a warm blanket, while below her the stillness of the hidden garden was disturbed only by the rasping of cicadas.

And beyond, in the bay, she could see the lights of the boats challenging the stars as they rode at anchor, dominated by the looming grandeur of *Persephone*.

No matter where I turn, she mused wryly, Vassos Gordanis seems to be dominating the picture.

But he'd chosen an odd name for his yacht, she thought, recalling the stories of the Greek myths she'd read at school. Persephone, if memory served, had no connection with the sea. She'd been a springtime goddess captured and carried off by Hades, the dark god of the Underworld, while she was picking flowers.

'A classic example,' her teacher Miss Gordon had said, 'of being in the wrong place at the wrong time.'

As a result of Persephone's abduction, so the story went, her mother Demeter was in such grief that she forbade the crops to grow until her daughter came back to her.

So Zeus, the supreme deity, decreed that Persephone should be returned to earth, as long as she had nothing to eat or drink while she was in Hades' power.

Only one day she'd found her favourite fruit—a pomegranate—in a dish on the table and eaten six of its seeds, enough to condemn her to spend half of each year in the Underworld. While the earth above stayed cold and barren, only coming back to life with her return for six months each spring.

'Which is,' Miss Gordon told them, 'a nice, convenient explanation for the annual change in the seasons.'

At the time, a much younger Joanna had mused wistfully that if Persephone had only managed to resist the temptation of the pomegranate altogether it would have been summer all the year round, with no frozen knees on the hockey pitch, chilblains, or horrible colds.

Now, with a swift wry smile at her own naïveté, she turned to go back into the suite, pausing with a gasp as she realised her way was blocked by a tall, lean and quite unmistakable figure lounging in the doorway.

Joanna took an instinctive step backwards. She said huskily, 'I—I didn't know anyone was there.'

The question *Why have you followed me?* was also hovering on her lips, but she bit it back. It was his suite, after all, and his balcony. And very soon it would be his hotel, too, so he could go where he pleased.

But it disturbed her that she'd been totally unaware of his presence, and especially that, while his face was shadowed, he could see her plainly in the light emanating from the room. And once again found herself cursing how little she was wearing.

Ridiculous, she thought with sudden breathlessness, to feel so exposed, so vulnerable, yet she did—even though Denys was within earshot.

He said softly, 'Forgive me for having startled you, *thespinis.*' He paused. 'It's a beautiful night, *ne?*'

She said, 'I—I just needed some air.'

He nodded. 'You find the atmosphere in the room tense, perhaps. It is understandable—when there is so much at stake.'

'Really?' She lifted her chin. 'I'd have said play has been quite moderate.'

'So far,' he said. 'But the evening has hardly begun. And, after all, so much depends on you, *thespinis.*'

'What do you mean?'

'You are Kyrios Vernon's lucky charm. He has said so.'

She bit her lip. 'Denys doesn't need a mascot. He's a very good player.'

'I think he will need to be.' Another pause. 'But I came to tell you that your drink is waiting.' He added softly, 'And that is a circumstance, perhaps, the only one, when the ice should not melt too soon.'

The words seemed to tingle over her skin in some strange way.

She swallowed. 'Is—is the game about to restart?'

'Yes,' he said, after a pause. 'It is getting late and I think we should waste no more time.'

He stood aside courteously to allow her to pass, but Joanna hesitated, reluctant to reduce the distance between them by so much as an inch.

Eventually she forced herself to move, edging past him, eyes on the ground, hoping her anxiety had not been recognised. Because it might amuse him, and she remembered his smile only too well, she told herself, renewed unease quivering in her senses.

No matter how many signals I may get from Dad, she thought as she went back into the suite, I cannot come on to Vassos Gordanis. He disturbs me in a way that has nothing to do with his being the richest man I've ever met.

And it doesn't involve him lusting after me, either, because he isn't the one who can't keep his eyes off me. He leaves that to the paid staff. Besides, I can usually recognise that response from men and I've learned to cope, if necessary.

Though not always with the greatest success, a small voice in her head reminded her, at least not in Australia.

I just know there's something else about him, she told herself restively, pushing the unbidden memory away. Something that I've never encountered before, and can't fathom. Some facet I don't even want to know about.

Please, she thought passionately, releasing her pent-up breath. Please let it all be over soon, so I never have to see him again.

All the players had changed seats during the break, her father included, but to her dismay Joanna found she was once again stationed directly opposite Vassos Gordanis.

She reached for her glass, and gulped down some of the

promised water, thankful for its refreshing chill against the dryness of her throat. And the ice was still intact, she thought, recalling his odd remark. It hadn't melted too soon at all.

Don't think about him, she told herself. Concentrate on the play.

She soon realised that her father's forecast that the stakes would be getting higher was fully justified.

The first pot, won by the South African Hansi Dorten with a straight, was worth over three thousand dollars, and she was relieved that Denys had decided to fold when the draw did not improve his original pair of tens.

But in the next hand his cards yielded a spade flush. There was a flurry of betting, then Chuck, Hansi and one of the Frenchmen all folded. But Vassos Gordanis, Henri de Morvan and Denys did not, each of them continuing to call and raise until there were over twenty thousand dollars' worth of chips in the middle of the table.

Joanna's hands curled into tense fists. This was it, she thought. The amount they needed to get them out of here, and some to spare. Make or break.

A second later it was all over. Vassos Gordanis shrugged ruefully, and tossed his cards towards the dealer, and Henri de Morvan followed suit.

Joanna watched Denys rake the chips towards him, her heart somersaulting. She had to bite the inside of her lip to stop a sheer grin of exultation spreading across her face. Because she didn't want any of these people, least of all the dark man sitting opposite, to know how much this mattered. How vital this was for her future. For everything.

She put her hand on her father's arm, pressing it warningly. Stop now, she urged silently. It's a big enough win, so make an excuse, cash in your chips and we'll get out of here.

But Denys was already selecting chips for the next game.

'Denys.' She lowered her voice to a whisper, her fingers tightening on his sleeve. 'Why don't we call it a night now—and celebrate?'

He glanced at her impatiently, ignoring the pleading in her eyes. 'Don't be silly, sweetheart. Your magic is working, and I'm on a winning streak, so we're going nowhere.'

But you promised, she wanted to cry aloud. You promised—you know you did....

And remembered too late that he'd sworn once before that she would never again have to use her eyes, her smile and her young body to divert another man's attention from the game, and how soon his word had been broken.

Or she would not be here, half-dressed, at this moment.

She sat, almost sick with fear, while the hand was played, but all the others folded after the draw this time, leaving Denys with another two thousand dollars to add to his winnings.

He sent her a triumphant wink as he prepared for the next game.

'Third time lucky, darling,' he muttered.

Then make this the last, Joanna implored silently. Please—please, Daddy. Quit while we're ahead.

I've never felt like this before, she thought. When he's been as confident as this, I've been right there with him. But maybe I've never been quite so disillusioned with my life before.

Yet in her heart she knew that wasn't it. That ever since *Persephone* had arrived in the bay and her father had announced his plans her every instinct had been screaming in warning.

And nothing that had happened since had done anything to reassure her.

She had learned to show no emotion, so her face was still, her eyes shuttered and her hands clasped loosely again in her lap as she saw Denys had been dealt a pair of kings and a pair of nines, with a small club as his fifth card. He discarded the club, asking for one, and received in return from the dealer the king of diamonds.

Three of a kind and a pair, Joanna thought, her heart beginning to pound. Full house. Good—but good enough? I just don't know.

The two Frenchmen folded quickly, but Hansi Dorten and Chuck briskly pushed up the betting, with Vassos Gordanis and Denys matching each call and raise.

Joanna reached for her glass and swallowed the remaining water as the pile of chips in front of her father began to diminish with startling speed.

'I'm out,' Chuck said wryly in answer to the South African's call and raise of five thousand.

'Fold,' Joanna whispered under her breath when it was Denys's turn to bet. 'Remember why you're here doing this, and leave us with something.'

Only to watch, helplessly, as her father pushed another pile of chips into the middle of the table and called.

'I also know when to stop,' Hansi Dorten said, tossing his hand on to the discard pile.

Vassos Gordanis counted out the requisite chips and added them to the pot. 'Call,' he said quietly. His hand moved again. 'And raise another ten thousand.'

Joanna was trembling inside. Showdown, she thought. The point of no return. Denys and Vassos Gordanis facing each other across the table, and between them—what? Thirty thousand dollars? Forty thousand? More?

Small change to a millionaire. The world to us. Or it could have been.

Because Dad hasn't enough left now for another call. Not at this kind of limit. He's been squeezed out. And we're wiped. We won't even be able to cover the bill for the suite.

Vassos Gordanis leaned back in his chair. 'What do you wish to do, *kyrie?*' It was a courteous, almost bland question.

Denys squared his shoulders. 'Naturally bet again, Mr Gordanis, if you are prepared to accept my IOU.'

The dark gaze looked past him with faint enquiry, and Joanna realised, startled, that Gaston Levaux had come back into the room, and was leaning against the wall, shaking his head in grim negation.

'I think our good Levaux doubts that you would have the ability to pay this debt if, of course, it falls due.' Vassos Gordanis reached pensively for another cheroot and lit it. 'However, there is a good deal of money at stake, and I wish to be fair. So I will give you the opportunity to back your hand once more—but only once. Therefore, you may call, and you may also raise me to whatever limit you wish and I will match it. Double the raise. Treble it, if you please. It is of no consequence.'

Denys stared at him, frowning. 'I don't take you for a philanthropist, Mr Gordanis, and I am not a charity case.'

'No,' the other returned softly. 'We are both gamblers, are we not? So, if you win, you take the money. All of it. There will be no dispute. I say it in front of witnesses.'

Joanna risked a swift glance round the table. The other men were very still, looking down unsmilingly at the table in front of them, but there was a tension in the air that was almost tangible.

'And if I lose?' Her father's voice was hoarse.

Vassos Gordanis shrugged. 'Then the money will be mine, naturally,' he returned levelly.

His eyes, brilliant as jet, and as cold, rested on Joanna, and she felt a tremor of awareness bordering on fear shiver through her body, as if cold fingers had trailed a path down her spine.

'But,' he added musingly, 'you would also owe me the amount you have wagered, and I would require that to be repaid.'

'And how could I possibly do that?' Denys flung at him.

'Not in cash, certainly.' He drew reflectively on his cheroot. 'But—in kind. That would be a different matter.'

'What the hell do you mean?' Denys demanded aggressively.

'I am wondering how much you are prepared to risk, Kyrios Vernon.' He nodded at Joanna. 'The beauty at your side, for instance. This girl—your charming talisman. How much do you consider she is worth to you?'

He leaned forward suddenly, and Joanna recoiled instinctively as she suddenly realised how right she was to have been afraid. And how much there still existed to terrify her.

'Because that is the pledge I require, my friend,' Vassos Gordanis went on, looking now at her father. 'In full and final settlement. If you play and lose, you give me the girl, and when she comes to me I take her for as long as I want her.' He paused. 'I also ask that you give me your word you will honour your debt as I have done, in front of witnesses,' he added almost casually.

As if, Joanna thought, a bubble of hysteria welling up inside her, he was attaching a postscript to a letter.

She wanted to protest. To scream at them all that she would never—never—submit to such a shameful bargain. That there was no amount of money on earth that could persuade her, either. That she would rather skivvy in the hotel, washing dishes or cleaning rooms, until their accommodation was paid for. Or starve in the gutter if she could get no work.

And, most of all, she wanted to tell them that Denys was not some kind of sugar daddy, as they apparently assumed, nor her pretended uncle—but her own real father, who would protect her with his life if need be.

Yet the ensuing silence was like a hand placed over her mouth. Her lips parted to speak but no sound emerged.

She would have given anything to get to her feet and storm out of the room in disgust, but all her energy seemed to have drained away, leaving her feeling as if she'd been nailed to the chair, unable to move so much as a hand in her own defence.

And if I tried to leave, she thought suddenly, would it be allowed?

Denys was speaking coldly, 'I presume, Mr Gordanis, that this is some crude and sordid joke.'

'And I have to tell you, Kyrios Vernon, that I am not joking,' Vassos Gordanis retorted. 'The money is there for the taking, by one of us. If you wish to fight for it, you must wager the girl. It is quite simple.' He shrugged again, his mouth twisting sardonically. 'But of course you do not have to accept my offer. You may prefer to fold and go on your way. Or you can be as serious as I am myself by naming your own figure and gambling on the cards you hold. Unless you have lost faith in the hand you have been defending?'

'No,' Denys denied thickly. 'I have not.'

Joanna felt as if she'd turned to ice. No? she thought almost blankly. Had she really heard him say no?

Because surely that had to be her response, as in—No, this cannot be happening.

Her father couldn't be contemplating playing on. It wasn't possible. He couldn't be staking her immediate future—her happiness—her innocence—on that kind of flimsy chance.

Even if he'd held a virtually unbeatable Royal Flush he shouldn't consider it. Not if he loved her…

Slowly she turned to stare at her father, willing him to look back, to meet the disbelief, the agony in her eyes, although instinct told her he would not.

Even my mother, she thought, anguished, always came second to this addiction—this monster eating away inside him. I think that in my secret heart I've always known that, so why did I ever imagine he'd be different with me?

She tried to say something. To beg for a reprieve—if not from Denys then from their adversary, who sat waiting, his face an expressionless bronze mask as the silence seemed to stretch into eternity.

Eventually, Denys spoke. 'I call,' he said hoarsely. 'And I raise—five hundred thousand.'

Vassos Gordanis looked at him, his brows lifted. 'Trying to scare me off, *kyrie?*' he enquired mockingly. 'I fear you will not do so. In fact, I am even more eager now to discover what could make her worth so high a price.'

He gestured imperatively, and the stout man approached and put a chequebook and pen on the table in front of him.

As if in a trance, Joanna watched him write the cheque and sign it, then place it with the pile of chips.

'I call,' he said, and sat back.

Denys put down his hand, face upwards. 'Full house,' he said. 'With kings.'

There was a pause, then Vassos Gordanis sighed, and lifted one shoulder in a philosophical shrug.

Bluffing, Joanna thought, a wild hope building inside her. He's been bluffing and Daddy's known it all along.

Hardly breathing, she watched their adversary turn his cards over. Saw the queen of diamonds go down, followed by the queen of clubs, to be joined next by the queen of spades.

He's got a full house too, she thought, her throat tightening in excitement and sheer relief as he put down his next card, the five of clubs. Queens and fives, which Dad's kings will beat. So I'm safe.

Only to see his long fingers place the last card on the table. A red card, depicting a woman holding a flower.

Joanna looked at it and the world stopped. Four of a kind, she thought numbly. Oh, God, he has four of a kind.

'The queen of hearts,' Vassos Gordanis said softly. 'So I win. Everything.'

And smiled at her.

CHAPTER FOUR

IT WAS, she thought, like being enclosed in a glass case. A place where she could see what was happening but take no part in it, and where her voice could not be heard.

Aware, but isolated. But still able to think. To reason.

The queen of hearts...

At first she told herself that it must be a joke. That no one could possibly win another human being for a bet, however large.

Sooner or later, she thought painfully, this ghastly humiliation would come to an end, and she and her father would be allowed to leave, even if all they took with them was their freedom to do so. Because they were in worse trouble than they'd ever been in their lives, as Gaston Levaux's tight-lipped presence only confirmed.

We don't just owe the hotel, she realised. There's also Mrs Van Dyne, who may not be very happy when she finds out what a total mess we're in.

But I mustn't think like that. When we're out of here, we can work something out. Denys will bounce back somehow, as he always does. I'm sure of it. I'll really ask Monsieur Levaux to find me a job in the kitchens or as a chambermaid. Something. Anything. And we'll survive. We always have before.

She forced herself to lift her chin, trying to appear unconcerned as she focussed once again on the events taking place in front of her. Trying, also, to ignore a cold, sick feeling in the pit of her stomach as she saw Vassos Gordanis reach for his cheque and quite deliberately tear it into small pieces, before placing the fragments in his ashtray and setting fire to them.

As she observed him summon Gaston Levaux and issue low-voiced instructions which she could not hear, but which, some instinct warned, concerned Denys and herself.

As she watched the other players get to their feet, shaking hands with their host and each other, but avoiding even a sideways glance at her or at her father, who remained motionless in his chair, his head buried in his hands.

Behaving, she thought, in a way that suggests they're too embarrassed to acknowledge our continuing presence in the room.

And she began to realise, as fear stirred within her, that the outcome of the evening might not be as simple as she'd hoped, or tried to believe.

As Chuck passed her, she impulsively caught at his sleeve. 'Help me.' Her voice was a thread. 'Help me—please.'

'Nothing doing, honey.' He detached himself firmly from her clasp. 'I'm a married man, and I know what my wife would say if I turned up with a cute little number like you.' He paused. 'Besides, if you can't stand the heat, you should've stayed out of the kitchen.'

But I didn't choose to be in the kitchen, she thought as she watched him leave with the others and turned to her father, who was still sitting, slumped in defeat.

Do something, she cried out to him in silent desperation. Say something. Stop all this now. Because you can't let it happen to me. You can't…

She saw Gaston Levaux approach him, accompanied by one of the quiet men from the Gordanis entourage. Saw them help him to his feet, making him walk between them to the door. Away from her. Abandoning her to the mercy of this stranger on the other side of the table. Which could well be no mercy at all.

And, somehow, she managed at this moment of crisis to find her voice at last.

'Don't go.' It was almost a scream as she jumped to her feet, preparing to follow. 'Don't leave me. Please…'

She saw Denys turn and look back at her, his face grey, his eyes hopeless in a way she'd never known before.

He has to tell them, she thought wildly. He has to tell them the truth about me. Gaston Levaux isn't a bad man. When he knows I'm Denys's daughter, and not his niece or something worse, he'll talk to this Vassos Gordanis. Make him see reason. Make him understand that he has to let me go.

I'll go after them—talk to Monsieur Levaux myself. Persuade him to help…

She took two steps towards the door, only to be halted in her tracks by a bulky figure in front of her.

'Your time with the man Vernon is over, *thespinis*.' It was the stout man, his face unsmiling, who'd detained her. 'You must forget him and understand that you belong now to Kyrios Gordanis.'

'No.' She tried to dodge past him, intent on reaching the outside corridor and finding her father, refusing to be parted from him, but he was immovable. 'I don't belong to him or anyone else—and I never will,' she added, flinging the words at Vassos Gordanis, who was still lounging in his chair, his cheroot held in his long fingers.

He looked back at her, his face impassive. 'You speak as if the choice was ever yours to make,' he retorted coldly. 'Now, go quietly with Stavros. I have no wish to force you.'

The threat of it was enough to quell her, temporarily at least.

With a sob of pure fright, she allowed herself to be ushered away, conducted into an adjoining room, lavishly appointed with sofas, chairs and occasional tables. However, her escort led her across it without pause, and through another door into the bedroom beyond.

'You will wait here,' she was brusquely instructed. 'And

before he comes to you, Kyrios Gordanis requires that you go to his bathroom and wash the make-up from your face.'

Joanna wrenched herself free. 'Tell him I'll do nothing of the kind,' she said hoarsely. 'And that he can go to hell.'

He gave her a sour smile. 'Tell him that yourself, *thespinis*—if you are brave enough. But I do not advise it. You are here to obey his wishes, not defy them. It will be better for you to remember that.'

He turned and left, closing the door behind him.

She sank to her knees on the thick carpet, hugging her arms round her trembling body.

She'd never experienced this feeling before. Even during that terrible time in Australia she'd always known that her father would keep her safe. That nothing bad would happen to her.

Only the fragile cornerstone of her security had been removed, and her entire world was tottering on the edge of disaster.

As the minutes dragged past, she lifted her head slowly and looked around her, taking reluctant stock of her surroundings.

It was a large room, elegantly furnished in the Empire style, and dominated by the widest bed she had ever seen. The coverlet was deep blue quilted silk and had been turned down on both sides, revealing white linen sheets and plump, frilled pillows.

As she assimilated this, Joanna felt physically sick, realising all the chilling personal implications of what she saw. The dire consequences of that last reckless bet which had delivered her into the power of a man like Vassos Gordanis.

As she recognised, too, that no one was going to put a hand on her shoulder and say Wake up. You're having a bad dream.

Her worst nightmare was about to become reality, and there was nothing she could do, and no one she could turn to.

Because a man whose existence she hadn't been aware of

before today was going to walk into this room at any moment and claim the kind of intimacies she'd thought she would only share with someone she both knew and loved. Someone that in all probability she was going to marry.

Now, instead of tenderness, she would be subjected to a man's demands for raw passion. And nothing in her life so far had prepared her for this. On the contrary…

She drew a quivering breath. She knew, of course, the basics of what would be expected of her. She was neither ignorant, nor completely stupid, having sat through the embarrassment of sex education classes. But her actual experience had never proceeded beyond a few tentative kisses.

And there'd only been that one encounter that she'd found even remotely threatening, and even then Denys's approach down the moonlit garden, his voice calling to her, had provided her with instant protection from kisses that had suddenly become too rough and hands that had tried, with clumsy determination, to grope at her shrinking body.

And if those fairly trivial advances had repelled her, how could she possibly cope with the prospect of being possessed completely? Used by a man for his casual pleasure then discarded?

She could feel a knot of misery tightening in her chest. She was more alone than she had ever been in her life and tears were not far away.

But she would not allow herself to shed them, she thought, as she scrambled up from the floor.

She was damned if she was going to behave like a victim, she told herself with stormy resolution. When Vassos Gordanis eventually decided to put in an appearance, she'd be on her feet and facing him with the contempt and disgust he deserved.

Because, whatever happened with the other women who crossed his path, he would fail with her. He might have won her at cards, but that would be his only victory. He wouldn't even have the satisfaction of hearing her plead. Instead, she would confront him with her total indifference.

And when he realised he was wasting his time and let her go, she would approach Monsieur Levaux and ask him to ring her uncle and arrange for her father and herself to return to England.

Where she would pretend that nothing had happened to her. That the outcome of the game had merely been another kind of bluff.

Only it wasn't, of course, she thought slowly. Looking back, she had the odd conviction that the entire evening had been planned to end exactly in that way. As if Vassos Gordanis knew her father's weaknesses as a gambler and had deliberately exploited them.

But that's not possible, she told herself. Neither of us has ever set eyes on him before yesterday. I know that. My God, if we'd met before I'd have remembered—and made sure I avoided any second encounter.

At the same time, she found her mind being drawn unwillingly back to the scruffy pirate who'd sent her that laughing salute from his deck some lifetime ago, trying to equate him with the hard-mouthed man who'd looked at her in cold triumph as he put down the winning card, but failing totally.

If he was still the pirate, she thought, maybe I could talk to him. Because, however aggravating, he'd seemed—almost human.

And halted, her mouth twisting in self-derision.

Are you crazy? she asked herself. We're not talking about some nicer twin brother here. Vassos Gordanis is one person, not two. And if he had an atom of decency or humanity about him you wouldn't be in this situation.

The room suddenly felt airless and she went over to the French windows, pulling the blue drapes aside and opening one of the glazed doors.

The night was cooler now, she discovered as she leaned against the doorframe. She drew several deep breaths, trying to calm herself, but it wasn't easy with *Persephone* there, right bang in front of her.

She bit her lip. There seemed to be nowhere she could go to escape its owner, either mentally or physically, she thought bitterly.

And although the story of the girl being carried off to Hell was only a legend, invented thousands of years ago, in Joanna's own mind right now it was beginning to take on a kind of dreadful reality.

Like Persephone of ancient days, she was being taken from everything and everyone she knew and loved, by a man of whom she knew nothing except that he had the money and power to do pretty much as he chose.

I wanted my life to change, she thought, swallowing. Wanted to escape. But not like this. Never like this.

Then, in the stillness, she heard the rattle of the door handle and knew that her temporary reprieve had come to an end. That she was no longer alone.

Hands clenched into fists at her sides, she made herself turn slowly and look at him.

He came forward slowly, tossing his dinner jacket and black tie across the dressing stool, and halted to regard her in turn, hands on hips, his gaze almost dispassionate.

He said, 'You were told to wash your face, but I see that you have not done so.'

Joanna lifted her chin. 'I don't take orders from strangers.'

'But we are not destined to remain strangers, you and I.' He began without haste to unfasten the remaining buttons on his shirt. 'As you very well know. Therefore you would be wise to obey me, and do as you have been told.'

'Why should I?' she challenged.

'Because I require it,' he said flatly. 'I was told you were beautiful, but that is impossible to judge when you hide yourself beneath a layer of scented grease.'

Told? she thought dazedly. Who told you—and why?

'It is surprising, too,' he added drily, 'when your choice of clothing, by contrast, leaves so little to the imagination.'

'You disapprove of the way I dress?' she asked defiantly. 'Under the circumstances, isn't that a little hypocritical?'

'I am talking of how you present yourself to others,' he said. 'What you wear for my eyes alone will be an entirely different matter. So go and wash.' He paused. 'Unless you wish me to do it for you.'

She said swiftly, 'That's the last thing I want.'

'Truly?' he asked mockingly, sending his shirt to join his other clothes on the stool. 'I thought—under the circumstances—you would have other far more serious objections to my plans for you.'

Her resentment of his high-handedness was indeed the least of her worries, she thought, swallowing.

At close quarters, stripped to the waist, he looked even more formidable, the dark hair on his chest tapering into a deep vee which disappeared into the waistband of his pants.

Nor, she realised, dry-mouthed, had she overestimated the muscled strength of his shoulders and arms. It suddenly seemed far wiser, if she could make her legs obey her, to make the small placatory gesture of going to the bathroom to do as he asked.

There was no facial cleanser among the toiletries on offer, just soap and water which did little to remove her eye make-up and left her looking like a bush baby.

The mirror above the basin told her that he had followed her, and was leaning in the doorway, observing her efforts with cynically raised eyebrows.

She drained the water and turned defensively to face him. He walked across to her and took her chin in his hand, the dark eyes examining her for an endless minute. She saw his brows lift as if he was surprised at something. And not pleased.

But all he said was, 'A slight improvement,' then moved away from her, casually unzipping his pants and discarding them. He reached into the shower and turned it on, then, to her horror, stripped off the black briefs that were his only covering and stepped calmly into the cubicle, letting the flow of water cascade over his naked body.

For a second Joanna was motionless, caught between shock and sheer embarrassment, then she gave a panic-stricken gasp and flew back into the bedroom, bent on flight, in case he should decide to summon her back to join him.

But having reached the door she stopped. Because how far did she expect to get, when everyone in the suite beyond was in his pay?

It seemed that the only means of escape left to her was by way of the window. And as this suite was on the hotel's top floor, that would mean instant oblivion.

She shivered as she went out on to the balcony to check that there was no climbing shrub or convenient drainpipe that might at least give her access to a lower floor. But there was nothing.

A fate worse than death, she thought, looking over the rail into the darkness beneath. Wasn't that the famous—and totally ludicrous—cliché? Because flinging herself down into infinity would never be an option for her, however scared she might be.

But I'm going to survive, she told herself. And choose another very different cliché. Where there's life, there's hope.

I will get through this, she thought, no matter what he does. Because none of it will be happening to me, but to the stranger who wears sexy clothes and too much make-up. The girl I've always detested. And I'll keep the real Joanna Vernon, the girl with hopes and dreams of an independent future, somewhere safe where Vassos Gordanis will never find her.

But there was still bewilderment under the brave resolution. Because if all he required was the novelty of an unfamiliar female body for a few hours, he surely he didn't have to go to these lengths to get what he wanted.

Even without the lure of his millions, there were probably women in the world who might well be attracted by his particular brand of masculinity, even if she would never be one of them.

How could he do that? she wondered, pressing her hands to her burning cheeks. How could he just—strip off in front of her as if she didn't matter—as if she wasn't even there?

Was that really the way a man would behave with a girl he planned to seduce?

Or was it another deliberate insult? A succinct demonstration of how lowly a place she occupied in his scheme of things.

If so, why had he gone to all that trouble and risked all that money in order to acquire her? Because he certainly hadn't been carried away by some passionate and irresistible desire.

When he'd touched her for the first time just now his fingers had been firm rather than caressing.

In fact, I'm not convinced that he really fancies me at all, she told herself. In which case, why—*why* am I here?

I was told you were beautiful...

Was that really enough to attract the attention of a man who could afford to buy anything and cause him to track her down?

If so, he must be seriously disappointed now that he had seen her. Perhaps he was already regretting that he'd wasted his time on such unpromising material, and her approaching ordeal would not be prolonged.

You don't matter to him, she whispered silently. And he will never matter to you. Remember that, and you will one day be able to forget this and regain your own life.

She took a deep breath and, head bent, walked slowly back into the lamplit room.

'It is a long way down, *ne?*'

The sound of his voice made Joanna start and come to an abrupt halt. She looked apprehensively across to where he stood, framed in the bathroom doorway, his expression faintly ironic as he watched her. He was wearing one towel draped round his hips, and drying his tousled black hair with another.

Even though he was marginally more covered than before, he still had far too much bronze skin on display, she thought, focussing her gaze on to the floor as heated colour rose in her face again.

'Consider, too, the feelings of the unfortunate who would have to remove what was left of you from the pathway,' he added.

'Don't worry,' she returned curtly. 'I had no intention of jumping.'

'Or of looking at me directly, it seems.' He sounded faintly amused. 'But why run away so coyly, *thespinis* ? I am made no differently from any other man.'

I'll have to take your word for that, she told him silently, her flush deepening. Because you're the only one I've ever seen naked.

Aloud, she said, 'Perhaps I simply prefer—any other man.'

'That is, of course, a possibility,' he said musingly. 'Yet my lack of clothing did not seem to disturb you while you watched me through your telescope.' His smile mocked her. 'Or did you think I would not recognise you once your face was clean?'

'I was admiring the boat,' she said curtly, hating him. 'Your presence was—incidental.'

'You had no premonition, Joanna *mou,* that we would encounter each other again—and so soon?'

'If I had,' she flung back at him, 'I would have made sure I was long gone.'

'You would not have got far without money.' He tossed aside the towel he'd been using on his hair, and walked to the dressing table, picking up a comb. 'Besides, my friend Levaux would not have permitted you to leave.'

'Of course,' she said. 'He would have to obey the new owner's orders.'

'You are premature,' he said. 'The deal has yet to be finalised. That is the other reason I am here.'

At that, she did look at him. She said, her breath catching, 'So it's not my imagination. You did plan all this.'

'Why, yes,' he said softly. 'And my plan succeeded better than I could have hoped. I, too, like to gamble for high stakes, but I can afford to lose.' He paused. 'Unlike the man Vernon, who took the bait, as I was told he would, and is ruined as he deserves.' He added, 'He has the bitterness, also, of knowing that his woman now belongs to me, so he has lost everything.'

'How could you do such a thing?' Joanna asked, her voice shaking. 'What kind of barbarian are you?'

'A rich one,' he said flatly. 'And one whom it is unwise to cross—unless you are prepared to suffer the consequences. But perhaps, *thespinis,* you thought you were immune—you and your companion.'

'How could I possibly have crossed you?' she protested. 'Twenty-four hours ago I—I didn't know you existed.'

'Whereas I have been aware of you for the past year,' he said. 'And looked forward to our meeting. I do not think I shall be disappointed.'

The dark eyes went over her. Slowly and quite deliberately stripping her naked, she realised dazedly.

'Please me,' he went on, 'and you will find me generous.'

She said thickly, mind and body recoiling, 'And if I don't please you?'

He shrugged, and her throat tightened as she watched, as if mesmerised, the play of muscle under the smooth skin of his shoulder.

'Then you will learn to do so, and quickly,' he returned almost indifferently. 'You have no other option, as I am sure you will come to see when you have considered the matter further.' He paused. 'And you will have time to do so. Your clothes and other possessions have already been packed, and tonight you will be flown to Greece, where you will wait for me on my island of Pellas.'

His slow smile made her shiver.

'I find anticipation increases the appetite—don't you?'

For a moment, shock held her mute. She'd thought that being made to surrender her virginity to him there on that bed was the worst that could happen to her. Had steeled herself to endure it. She had never expected—this.

When she could speak she queried hoarsely, 'You're—taking me to Greece? But you can't.'

'And what is there to stop me?'

'The law. Because it's kidnap.' Joanna flung back her head. 'And that's a criminal offence in any country.'

'You have a short memory, Joanna *mou*.' Hands on hips he regarded her, the dark face forbidding. 'You are forgetting that I won you from the man Vernon in a poker game in front of witnesses. If you objected to your body being wagered in such a way, you should have said so at the time.' He paused. 'You may cheat others, my girl, but do not try to do the same to me. It is too late for that. And Pellas is where I keep all my prized possessions—until, of course, they no longer have the value of novelty and begin to bore me.'

'And what—what happens then?' The words almost choked from her.

'I sell them,' he said. 'To a new owner.' He added softly, 'I expect you to bring me a handsome profit, my lovely one, when I have finished with you at last.'

CHAPTER FIVE

His words seemed to echo and re-echo through the silence that followed.

Joanna stared at him, almost giddy with horror and disbelief, trying to tell herself that he didn't—he couldn't—mean what he was saying.

But if he was trying to frighten her then he'd succeeded beyond his wildest dreams.

She said in a voice she did not recognise, 'Why are you doing this?'

'You have brought this upon yourself, *thespinis*.' There was renewed harshness in his voice. 'You have chosen to use your body to turn men into fools. You would have attempted to do the same to me earlier tonight, if I had allowed it. Do not bother to deny it,' he added contemptuously as her lips parted in shock. 'Your guilt is known. But now things have changed for you, and it is your turn to be used. Used, then discarded.'

'Whatever I did, I did for my—for Denys.' She managed to keep her voice steady, although her mind was whirling frantically. I was right, she thought. But how did he know so much? How?

'And he needs me,' she went on. 'So, I—I can't leave France. Can't leave him behind. And I—won't.'

'Your loyalty is touching, but misplaced, Joanna *mou*,' he said coldly. 'Is it possible you can still care about him, after what he has done?'

'I do more than care.' She lifted her chin defiantly. 'I love him, and I always will—whatever he does.'

'Then I hope for your sake that the English saying is wrong—and that absence does not make the heart grow fonder.' His tone was cynical. 'Because you will never see him again.'

She caught her breath. 'What have you done to him?' she queried hoarsely. 'Oh, God, you haven't—hurt him?'

For a moment he looked almost startled, then his mouth hardened. 'I did not have to,' he told her brusquely. 'He has damaged himself quite enough, I think, and must live with the consequences.' He paused. 'I wonder, too, how much your loss will really matter to him when he has so many other problems pressing on him. After all, one woman is very like another.'

She flinched from the callousness of the remark. 'You think that he'll simply let me go? That he won't come to find me? You're wrong.'

'But there would be no point,' he said gently. 'He will never again be able to afford you.' He paused. 'If he ever could.'

'Then at least let me see him—to say goodbye.' She was pleading unashamedly now. For her father the initial shock would be wearing off now, and she knew he would be guilt-stricken and desperate. How he'd react if she simply vanished—if he had no idea where she'd been taken—didn't bear thinking about.

For a moment she was tempted to tell Vassos Gordanis the truth. To say, He's not what you think—he's my father. Knowing what he's condemned me to will be the end of him.

But something kept her silent. Because the evening's disasters had involved far more than just a card game, she thought. There was real animosity seething below the surface and until she discovered its cause it might be better to keep quiet about her relationship to Denys in case it simply added fuel to the flames, she decided, repressing a shiver.

'Your goodbyes were said, Joanna *mou,* when he decided

to bet against me.' His voice was inexorable. 'And I think you will find me an adequate substitute for a man three times your age.' His smile mocked her. 'Who knows? You may even discover that you enjoy sharing my bed.'

Oh, God, he was so sure of himself, she thought, her inner chill turning to fury. So arrogantly certain that any girl would succumb eventually and welcome him as her lover. That he probably wouldn't even have to try...

'Never,' she said, her voice shaking. 'Never in this world. Because you are totally vile. Vile and—disgusting. And I hate you. Just the thought of having you touch me makes me feel physically sick. So please don't wait to pass me on to the next man. Sell me now, because I'd rather be with anyone else on earth than with you.'

His brows lifted. 'I would not be so sure,' he told her sardonically. 'Nor do you have the power to be selective about your future, *thespinis*. Like it or not, at the moment you belong to me, and I alone shall decide when to let you go and on what conditions. As I thought I had made clear.'

She stared at him. 'Why are you doing this? Because it makes no sense.' She drew a small, harsh breath. 'I don't believe you even like me, let alone—want anything from me.'

He shrugged again. 'As I remarked just now, Joanna *mou,* you come to me highly recommended. And now this discussion has gone on long enough,' he added, yawning, as her hands clenched involuntarily into fists at her sides at his cold-blooded retort. 'I have negotiations to conduct tomorrow. A deal to make, therefore I need to get some sleep.'

Sleep? In spite of herself, Joanna found her gaze turning to the bed, a quiver of apprehension running through her.

He noticed and laughed. 'No, *pedhi mou.* I cannot spare the time or energy for your kind of distraction just now, when I have business to transact. But when we meet again on Pellas you will have no cause to feel neglected, I promise you. You will make a most interesting diversion for my leisure hours.'

He walked to the door and called, 'Stavros.'

The door opened so promptly that Joanna wondered if the Gordanis chief dogsbody had been standing with his ear pressed to the panels.

Vassos Gordanis spoke to him quietly in Greek, and he nodded impassively and came over to Joanna, holding out the trench coat he was carrying over his arm.

'You will wear this, *thespinis,* if you please.'

'Why should I?' She squared her shoulders mutinously, putting her hands behind her back.

'Because I wish it,' Vassos Gordanis interposed, his tone level. 'Let this be your first lesson in obedience to me, Joanna *mou.* From now on you will dress and behave with modesty. Do you understand?'

'Yes,' she said. 'I understand.'

But you don't. Do you imagine that these clothes were my choice? That I liked pretending to be something I'm not? Something I never will be, no matter what happens?

She took the coat, which clearly belonged to someone male and very much larger who could even be Vassos Gordanis himself, she thought, shuddering inside, and put it on, tying the belt round her waist with an angry jerk to keep it in place.

Then she walked to where he was standing.

'I understand completely,' she went on, biting out the words. 'You appalling bloody hypocrite.' And she swung back her arm and slapped him across the face with such force that her shoulder felt jarred. But it was like punching a marble statue. Even taken off-guard, he did not move an inch, or as much as put a hand to his cheek where her finger marks were immediately and clearly visible.

He said quietly, 'You will pay for that insult when we meet again, *thespinis,* and in coin of my choosing that you may not like. Because we already have another score to settle, you and I. The matter of Petros Manassou. Or did you think you had got away with it?'

She cradled her stinging hand in the palm of the other, staring at him in open bewilderment. 'I don't know what you're talking about.'

'No?' There was a jeering note in his voice. 'Then think back, Joanna *mou*. You will have plenty of time to do so while you are waiting for me to come to you on Pellas.'

He watched the angry colour drain from her face and nodded, his mouth twisting in a smile that did not reach his eyes.

'Now go,' he directed curtly. 'And have the wisdom to learn some manners—and perhaps a little remorse—before our next encounter.'

He turned away and walked towards the bed, casually loosening the concealing towel as he went, and Joanna hastily spun in the opposite direction, heading blindly for the door, her teeth sinking painfully into her lower lip before she could be subjected to another glimpse of her persecutor naked.

In the room beyond she paused momentarily, steadying herself with a hand on the back of the sofa. *Another score to settle...*

Revenge, she thought, horrified, her mind reeling away from the implications of the night's discoveries. I'm being taken away for some kind of revenge. Nothing else.

In his own words—'used, then discarded'.

But why? she asked herself, her heart thudding painfully against her ribcage. What can I possibly have done to deserve this treatment from someone I'd never even heard of yesterday? There—there has to be some mistake.

Stavros touched her arm, urging her onwards, and she shook him off almost savagely.

The hired help could keep his hands to himself. It was enough to know that some time soon she would have to endure Vassos Gordanis' touch, and worse.

And seeing him without his clothes on a daily or nightly basis was probably the least of it. She'd avoided it this time, but it was something she'd have to deal with—when she had to, and not before.

Or *if* she had to…

Because she wasn't beaten yet, she thought with sudden determination as she pulled herself upright and began to walk slowly forward. Not by a long chalk.

Because she wasn't about to have her life ruined over some imagined wrong by a man with too much power for his own good.

She hadn't yet reached his yacht, or his wretched private island. She was still in a large hotel with a foyer which, even at this time of night, would not be deserted. Quite apart from the staff, there would be people there who could hardly ignore the sight and sound of a screaming girl being dragged kicking and struggling off the premises, and would surely feel bound to intervene.

And the reception staff could hardly stay aloof either, not if she was claiming at the top of her voice that she was being kidnapped. They'd do anything to avoid that kind of scandal, she told herself.

Which meant that Stavros, still doggedly at her heels, would have to let her go. He'd have no choice. And, once free, she would immediately demand that the police be called, and insist on being reunited with her father. After which, it would be that emergency call to Uncle Martin and a speedy departure.

And let Vassos Gordanis see where his bet stood then.

She might not have to wait to reach the foyer, she thought hopefully. Not if she could outrun the man behind her and get to the lift first. She'd find a refuge somewhere. Even if she couldn't immediately locate Denys, she knew that Chris and Julie would help her without hesitation. And no one would look for her there at their secluded bungalow.

It wouldn't be easy in these ridiculous high-heeled boots, but it was worth a try, she thought, taking a deep breath as they approached the door to the corridor, bracing herself for the attempt.

Only to find the man she'd last seen taking her father away

stepping forward as she emerged, and placing a firm hand on her arm.

'Let go of me.' She tried to pull away, but he was unyielding.

He looked past her. He said with cold civility. 'I have my instructions, *thespinis.*'

Then it would have to be her original plan after all, Joanna thought as she was marched briskly to the lift. The hysterical scene in the foyer. And wondered how loudly it was possible to scream if she really put her mind to it. I'll give it my best shot, she promised herself, tension twisting in the pit of her stomach. Because the alternative is unthinkable. Unbearable.

She stood quietly, staring into space, as the lift descended. She needed to make them think that she'd accepted the fate imposed on her. That she'd been stunned into submission.

Well, they would soon think again. And so would their revolting bastard of a boss who, with any luck, would be attending his meeting with a bruised face.

She cast a swift glance at the indicator panel, noting with satisfaction that they were nearing the ground floor, and waiting for the lift to slow down. Except that it wasn't doing anything of the kind, she realised, her heart skipping an alarmed beat. Instead, it was continuing downwards to the hotel basement.

She said huskily, 'What's happening? Where are we going?'

'To the entrance used by the staff.' It was Stavros who answered, his smile grim. 'Kyrios Gordanis decided it would offer more privacy.'

'No.' Panicking as her plan began to come apart at the seams, Joanna began to struggle. 'No, I won't leave like this. I won't. I have to go to Reception—speak to someone. Let them know I'm going.'

'All the necessary arrangements have already been made. The car is waiting to take us to the airport.'

'I won't go.' She kicked the man who was holding her. He

winced but did not release his grip. 'Leave me alone, damn you. You can't do this.'

'Kyrios Gordanis' order were quite clear, *thespinis*. Fighting will not help you. I advise calm.'

She said between her teeth, 'To hell with calm.'

As the lift stopped and the doors opened, Joanna opened her mouth in the hope of attracting attention. But before she could make a sound...

'I regret this necessity.' Stavros sounded almost gloomy. 'But you have brought it upon yourself.'

The next instant he'd hoisted her over his shoulder as if she was a roll of carpet and was carrying her, squirming but helpless, down the passage towards the metal door at the end.

She was crying with rage and frustration, but suddenly, absurdly, she was thankful, too, that her indecently minimal attire was at least covered by the trench coat.

Her kidnapper had thought of everything, she stormed inwardly. Stayed one jump ahead of her all the time, as if they'd known each other for years and he could read her mind.

They were outside now, following some narrow path which, she guessed despairingly, must lead down to one of the side gates. So any remaining hope she might have had that their progress might be challenged was fading fast.

Being carried along like this with her head dangling was increasing her feeling of nausea, so it was a genuine relief to be set on her feet again.

Stavros walked to the rear passenger door of a dark saloon car and opened it. 'Conduct yourself quietly, *thespinis,* and all will be well. We have no wish to shame you.'

Was he being ironic? Joanna wondered wildly. Or did he have no idea of the real shame awaiting her on Pellas?

For a long moment she hesitated defiantly, then, with a reluctant nod, got into the car, shrinking into the corner as Stavros joined her.

As the vehicle moved off, she allowed herself a last, brief assessment of her chances if she were to jump out, but decided

they were not worth considering. Even if the doors were un-
locked, she would simply be retrieved and they would drive
on.

No, she thought. Her best chance was to get away from
Pellas itself before its master returned.

Not everyone in the world would be falling over themselves
to do his bidding. Anyone as arrogant, autocratic and ruthless
was bound to have enemies, even on his private island.

All she had to do was find one of those enemies and promise a reward for her successful escape. Her father would not
be able to pay, but Uncle Martin surely would, although the
prospect of telling him and Aunt Sylvie about the turn her life
had taken since leaving England made her shrink inside.

But it was still better than the alternative, she reminded
herself grimly.

Anything was better than that.

She sat, her hands folded in her lap, staring out at the darkness, as she tried again to rationalise what had happened. To
work out why Vassos Gordanis had singled her out from the
rest of female humanity and was hell-bent on wrecking her
life in this hideous way.

And it wasn't enough to tell herself that he'd simply made
a terrible, disastrous mistake.

Another score to settle…

That was what he'd said.

Or did you think you had got away with it?

And he'd said something else—in Greek, although she'd
only picked up on the word *petros* which, she remembered
from her RE lessons, meant 'rock', as well as being a man's
name. A play on words, she thought. That was it.

'Thou art Peter and on this rock…'

And she stopped right there, with a sudden painful lurch
of the heart. For Petros, she thought, substitute Peter.

She closed her eyes, shivering. Because she'd only known
one Peter. The boy she'd met so briefly and disastrously in
Australia last year. Not all that tall, she thought, with hair

verging on sandy and dark brown eyes. Quite good-looking, and much too aware of it. Full of himself in other ways as well, constantly boasting about contacts, deals, and all the money he was carrying to make them.

Apparently convinced that he was irresistible, when staying at the same hotel and seeking her out constantly, he'd been simply—unavoidable.

But he'd been Peter Mansell, not Petros whatever it was, she argued desperately. And not Greek, either. He was from California. He'd said so, and his accent had seemed to confirm it.

The boy that, ever since, she'd done her best to forget.

'You've ruined me. You've cheated me—all of you.'

She remembered the overturned chair falling to the floor, and his voice, hoarse with despair. And frank terror.

'You can't do this. You have to give me a chance to win some back. Or I'm a dead man—don't you understand?'

And she hadn't been able to look him in the face, knowing that the only cheat in the room had been herself.

Total betrayal, she thought bitterly, recoiling from the memory. Judas in hot pants.

She'd lived with the shame of it ever since. And now, it seemed, there was worse shame to come.

Because she could suddenly remember exactly what Vassos Gordanis had said. A name—Petros Manassou.

For which, she supposed, Peter Mansell was a fair translation, if you were young and silly and wanted to pretend for some reason that you weren't Greek but a rich American.

Another score to settle…

Or did you think you had got away with it?

Oh, God, she thought. Oh, dear God, if I did, then I know better now. Because it's all caught up with me at last, and I'm going to be made to pay. And this time there's no way out for me.

And as the car sped through the darkness Joanna drew a

slow shaking breath and made herself remember how it had begun…

'You're a pretty girl.' That had been Diamond Lenny, his eyes appraising her through a cloud of cigarette smoke. 'And he's a flash kid with a wad of money who fancies the pants off you. So get to work on him, babe. Give him the hots until he can't see straight, let alone think, then lead him to us.'

'No, I won't.' Her protest had been immediate and instinctive, and she'd turned to her father, her eyes imploring. 'Please, Denys.' She'd stumbled over the still unaccustomed name. 'You can't want me to do this. Tell him so.'

'No, Denys, mate, you tell her.' Impatiently, Diamond Lenny stubbed out his cigarette. 'Advise your little sweetie on the economic facts of life. That the hotel rooms, the fancy tucker and the sexy gear all cost money, and it's time she did a bit more than show off her legs and bat her eyelids at the punters. Made a definite contribution, in fact.'

He sent her a lascivious grin. 'You're female. You know how to get a bloke all worked up, then prim up and back off while he's trying to get his zip down. But if things should go a bit too far…' He shrugged. 'Old Denys will forgive you, won't you, mate? Just as long as you get the boyfriend and his cash to the back room at Wally's Bar tonight.'

'I know Lenny can sound a bit rough,' Denys had said uncomfortably when they were alone. 'But he doesn't mean half of it.'

'I think he does,' Joanna said flatly. She swallowed. 'You really expect me to lead Peter Mansell on over dinner? Let him think that I'll—give in to him later, so that you and those crooks at Wally's can take him for every cent he has?' She shook her head. 'I—I can't believe you really mean it.'

'He's been asking for it—bragging about being loaded all over town,' Denys said defensively. 'If it isn't us, then someone else will have him. And Lenny's right. We need the money.' He patted her arm. 'You can trust me, my pet. I won't let anything happen to you.'

She didn't look at him. She didn't think she could bear to, she thought desolately, and knew that she wanted to cry.

'Very well,' she said at last, her voice toneless. 'I'll try and do as you want, on condition that you don't ask me to do anything similar for as long as I live. And that afterwards we don't see Lenny or any of his revolting friends ever again—even if it means moving to another continent.' She added quietly, 'Daddy, I mean it.'

And he'd assured her that it would be a one-off. An emergency situation calling for desperate measures.

And over dinner, provocatively dressed, she'd endured Peter Mansell's hand on her bare knee, and his hot eyes devouring her. Had gone out into the night-scented garden with him, and stood feeling physically repelled while his mouth greedily explored her neck, and his hand fumbled with the front of her shirt.

While she'd made herself tell him that, yes, she wanted this, too, but she couldn't. That they must stop because Denys would be looking for her. That there was a card game that night and she was his lucky mascot.

Then whispering, 'But you could always come with us. And maybe, if Denys has too much to drink, we'll find some way to be together later—afterwards...'

She knew now with utter certainty that it was useless trying to blame her predicament on the Persephone myth. Simply being, as Miss Gordon had said, in the wrong place at the wrong time. Catching the eye of the Dark Lord of the Underworld and being carried off with him to Hell.

Because chance had never been involved.

And the Hell waiting for her was no myth, but all too terribly real.

CHAPTER SIX

JOANNA would never forget her first glimpse of Pellas, looking down from the window of the Lear Jet—Vassos Gordanis would, of course, have to have a Lear Jet, she'd told herself bitterly—on what seemed little more than a splash of dark emerald in a restless azure sea.

It looked so tranquil, she thought. As if nothing bad could ever happen there. Proving once again how deceptive appearances could be.

Nor was it her idea of a Greek island, she thought with vague bewilderment. She'd imagined bleached rock, studded with the occasional ruined temple. Not all that—verdancy.

Stavros was now her sole escort, his companion having presumably gone back to the hotel to arrange another kidnapping, or whatever piece of criminality his boss had planned next. He'd informed her shortly after take-off that they would be landing on the neighbouring island of Thaliki, then completing their journey by boat.

He had then gone to sleep, but she could not. She was too tense, her mind plodding in weary, hopeless circles.

We must have been so easy to track down, Dad and I, she thought sombrely, for someone who was rich enough—and angry enough.

And it was the anger that was preying on her mind. The anger and the contempt that Vassos Gordanis had displayed towards Denys and herself. The cold-blooded resolution which had driven him on.

And, worst of all, the desire for revenge which would use sex as a punishment, destroying her self-respect along with her innocence.

They must all have been in on it, she thought with a pang. All his friends helping him—believing the worst of me. Making quite sure the trap would close on his intended victim.

But was it loyalty Vassos Gordanis inspired or merely fear?

Because she kept thinking of that other victim—the boy, his white face damp with sweat. His mouth twitching, his eyes flicking from side to side as he said, 'I'm a dead man.'

Surely, she thought shivering, surely he couldn't have meant that. It had to be a figure of speech. Didn't it?

Or was it possible that being so rich and so powerful could set a man like that above the norms of human behaviour? Make him believe he could take ruthlessness to its ultimate point? And make others believe it, too?

And she wondered exactly what had happened to his wife.

But stopped short, knowing that she was being absurd, because Vassos Gordanis was not a mass murderer.

For a moment she was assailed once more by the unwilling and disturbing memory of the first time she'd seen him, watching her with lazy appreciation from his deck. Someone without an apparent care in the world, let alone dark thoughts of vengeance.

But that, of course, was before he'd discovered who she was. Since then he'd been ahead of her every step of the way...

Except now, when she was going to his island alone—to wait for him.

It occurred to her that she didn't even know where Pellas was. Greece had so many islands, so she had no idea which group it might belong to, or whether it would be in the Aegean or the Ionian Sea.

Not that it mattered that much, she reminded herself flatly. It was rather like pondering whether you'd rather be hanged or beheaded. Because wherever this place might be, the nightmare she was due to face remained exactly the same.

And, like a sentence of death, there was no way out.

The boat from Thaliki was another surprise. She'd expected something sleek and streamlined to complement *Persephone,* not an elderly fishing boat with peeling blue paint, chugging doggedly to its destination.

It would almost be a relief to get there, she thought, easing her shoulders wearily inside the trench coat. She was dazed with her lack of sleep, and although it was still early every stitch she had on was sticking to her. Walking across the Tarmac to the single-storey shack which served Thaliki as a terminal, she'd felt as if she'd collided with a wall of heat.

And these vile boots seemed to have become a size smaller, too. They'd probably have to be cut off her, and good luck to them. She never wanted to see them, or anything she was wearing, ever again.

'See, *thespinis.*' Stavros came to stand beside her in the bow, pointing. 'The Villa Kore.'

She looked in the direction indicated and saw a thickly wooded hill. Rising above the greenery at its crown was a large house, painted white with a terracotta tiled roof.

She swallowed. 'Kore?' she queried. 'Is that the name of some god?'

'The name of a goddess, *thespinis,*' he corrected. 'In your language Villa Kore means the House of the Maiden—she who was the daughter of the Great Mother.'

Who, Joanna recalled, Miss Gordon had also mentioned in those mythology lessons. The once supreme Earth Goddess in all her many manifestations—from Gaia, who'd preceded the Titans and the other male gods, to Astarte, Isis, Cybele and, in Greece, Demeter.

'The mysteries of Eleusis.' She spoke the thought aloud. 'So the maiden must be Persephone.'

'You know of these things?' He sounded genuinely surprised.

'I went to school,' she said. 'Like everyone else.' *Because I wasn't born behaving like a tart at poker games, whatever your boss may think.*

She looked back at the island. They were approaching a long curving strip of pale sand sloping gently into the sea. At one side, where a wooden landing stage thrust out into the water, a small group of men stood waiting, a couple of them with rifles slung over their shoulders.

'The firing squad?' she asked lightly, wondering if it was appropriate to joke about it.

'Security,' he said. 'A few years ago a photographer got ashore on Skorpios and took pictures of Madame Onassis sunbathing without clothing. Since then Kyrios Vassos has made sure no intruders land here.'

Joanna had a dim recollection of the fuss in the papers when the nude pictures of the former Jacqueline Kennedy had been published in Italy.

She shrugged. 'Well, he needn't worry about me,' she said. 'If I choose to sunbathe, I shall not be emulating the beautiful Madame Onassis.'

'I think you have forgotten you belong to Kyrios Vassos, and will therefore do whatever he requires, *thespinis*.' His tone was flat. 'But modesty is not his chief concern in the matter. The man on Skorpios could have had a gun, not a camera.'

'So presumably I'll be watched, and my movements will be restricted.' She stared rigidly in front of her.

'By no means. You are a guest on Pellas, *thespinis*.' He spoke with faint reproof. 'You are free to go wherever you wish.'

'Presumably because there's nowhere to hide and no way off, either,' she said with bitter accuracy. She paused, reluctant to ask the question that was burning in her brain, but recognising it must be done. 'When—when will Mr Gordanis be arriving?'

'When his business is completed—and when he chooses,' was the flat retort. 'Two days—three days. A week—two weeks. Who knows? What does it matter? After all, *thespin- is,* as you have realised, you are going nowhere.'

And the faint triumph in his smile reminded her unerringly exactly who still held the winning hand.

She had braced herself for the inevitable curiosity when she stepped out on to the landing stage, but it did not transpire.

She could remember the previous autumn catching an epi- sode of a new TV series starring David McCallum called *The Invisible Man.* Well, now, she thought ruefully, she knew what it was like to be the invisible woman.

Because no one even glanced in her direction as Stavros escorted her along the planking to the flight of steps at the end. And, though they seemed more concerned with unpack- ing various sacks and boxes from the boat, something told her that they were quite deliberately averting their gaze.

But it was probably nothing personal. Perhaps they were under orders not to ogle any of the women that Vassos Gordanis brought here for his amusement, she told herself. Anyway, she had far more to worry about than that.

'Is it far to the house?' she asked, breaking a silence that threatened to become oppressive as she stepped carefully on to the beach, cursing her boots under her breath.

'Not when you are accustomed.' He paused. 'But the path is uneven, and your heels are not suitable. You must take care not to fall.'

'Oh, dear,' she said, poisonously sweet. 'Are you supposed to hand me over to the great man undamaged?'

'To Kyrios Vassos you are already damaged goods, *thes- pinis.* But you would find a broken ankle painful.'

Damaged goods... The words stung, and she longed to fling them back in his face—and the face of the man who now owned her. Tell *him* that he was so wrong about her. Except she would not be believed.

Biting her lip, she sat down on the step behind her and began to unlace her boots.

She sat for a moment, flexing her bare toes, then rose leaving the boots lying in the sand.

'You do not wish to take them with you, *thespinis?*'

'I never want to see them again.' *Or anything else I'm wearing.*

It was cooler under the canopy of trees, and Joanna took a deep breath of pine-scented air.

The track was just as rough as Stavros had warned, with stones and tree roots half-buried in the sandy soil, and she picked her way carefully, Stavros walking beside her.

'The Villa Kore is a fine house,' he commented eventually. 'It is where Kyrios Vassos was born, and he comes here to relax and enjoy his privacy.'

'I can imagine how,' Joanna returned coldly.

'The *kyrie* likes also to live simply,' Stavros went on, as if she hadn't spoken. 'So while there is a generator for electricity, communication is by radio, and there is no telephone on the island.' He added, 'He desires you to know this so that you will not waste time searching.'

Joanna, who'd planned to do exactly that, felt her heart sink.

'He also wishes for you to have every comfort, *thespinis*. It is safe to swim from the beach, or there is a pool at the house, if you prefer. Whatever else you require, you have but to ask.'

'I want only one thing,' she said swiftly. 'To be as far away from your Kyrios Vassos as it's possible to get on this earth.'

'Ah,' he said. 'You are thinking of Australia, perhaps.'

Joanna, flushing, subsided. Of course Stavros would know the reason behind his master's pursuit of an insignificant girl, she thought. But instinct warned her it would be futile to ask him. That the information would come only from Vassos Gordanis—if at all.

They turned a corner and Joanna saw a dazzle of sunlight

ahead. Fifty yards later and she was taking her first good look
at the Villa Kore.

It was larger than she'd realised—massive, even—but her
first thought was, it looks cold. An impression reinforced
by the blue shutters at all the windows like so many closed
eyes.

The surrounding gardens were oddly formal, too, with their
clipped lawns kept a vivid green by sprinklers, and the flow-
erbeds bright with blooms that appeared to have been planted
by numbers.

After the unspoilt beach and the clustering trees, it was like
crossing some barrier into a different world, Joanna thought,
wondering if anyone had ever run on that grass or kicked a
ball there.

Aware that she was being watched, she glanced back at the
house and saw that a burly man, neat in dark trousers and a
grey linen jacket, had emerged from the main entrance.

'Andonis Leftanou, *thespinis*,' Stavros informed her. 'He
is major-domo for Kyrios Vassos and waits to welcome you.
You should reply *efharisto*, which is Greek for thank you.'

'Except I don't feel very grateful.' Joanna gave him an icy
look. 'Maybe I should tell him instead that, when I get out of
here, I'm going to have your mutual employer charged with
kidnapping, and the pair of you arrested as accessories and
see how welcoming he is then.'

'Say what you wish, *thespinis*.' Stavros shrugged. 'It will
change nothing. To him you remain the guest of Kyrios Vassos,
to be received with courtesy.'

Andonis Leftanou's greeting was indeed polite, accompanied by a slight, dignified inclination of the head. But there
was no warmth in his voice, or in his brief smile. And, once
again, his eyes seemed to slide past her.

After the brilliance of the sun, the house seemed full of
shadows, and as she looked round the wide hallway Joanna
stiffened, aware of someone—a figure—standing in an alcove
at one side, watching, motionless and in silence.

She caught her breath. 'Who is that?'

Stavros followed the direction of her gaze. 'It is Kore, *thespinis*.' He sounded almost amused. 'Nothing more. Come, look.'

It was the life-size statue of a girl, carved in white marble, the face remote and lovely, the mouth curved in a half-moon smile. She wore the classic Greek *chiton,* falling in folds to her bare feet, and one hand was extended, palm upwards, offering a piece of fruit.

For a moment Joanna thought she was holding an apple, then she looked more closely and saw that it was actually a pomegranate.

Persephone, she thought. The Maiden Goddess. Trapped here, too, at the pleasure of the Dark Lord, with the fruit of her own betrayal in her hand.

'It is beautiful, *ne?*' Stavros prompted.

Joanna shrugged as she turned away, feeling oddly disturbed. 'If you like that kind of thing.' She paused. 'Now, perhaps you'll show me where I'm to be kept until your master arrives.'

He nodded curtly. 'Hara will take you there.' He signalled to the far end of the hall and a grey-haired woman in a dark dress, and wearing a starched apron, came forward.

She was built on impressively generous lines, with a plump face that looked as if it should have been merry, yet her expression was set and dourly unfriendly as she indicated wordlessly that Joanna should follow her to the wide flight of marble stairs.

She led the way along the gallery to a door at the end and flung it wide, gesturing to Joanna to precede her into the room.

Lifting her chin, Joanna obeyed, and paused, her eyes widening as she surveyed her new surroundings.

As rooms went, this one was pretty breathtaking, she admitted reluctantly. The gleaming satin bedspread covering the wide divan was patterned in green and gold, and those colours were repeated in the luxuriously quilted headboard, and the curtains that hung at the long windows.

The floor was tiled in ivory, and the range of fitted wardrobes and drawers that occupied an entire wall had been constructed from wood the colour of warm honey.

Hara crossed the room, still unsmiling, and opened a door revealing a cream marble bathroom, with a shower as well as a deep tub. Joanna swallowed deeply as she absorbed its perfection, from the gold- framed mirrors above the twin washbasins to the array of expensive toiletries and piles of fluffy towels waiting in mute invitation.

She supposed now, if ever, was the moment to use the *efharisto* word, but when she turned to speak the older woman had silently vanished, and she was alone.

Her first act was to check the wardrobes for male clothing, but they were empty, indicating to her relief that Vassos Gordanis usually spent his nights elsewhere. Or had done so in the past.

She walked across to the bed and tested the mattress with an experimental hand. Was it only yesterday that she'd longed to sleep on something even half as comfortable as this promised to be?

Yet now she would have given anything she possessed to be back at the hotel, facing another night on that penance of a sofa.

And even the knowledge that for the time being she would be sleeping alone was no consolation.

Green and gold, she thought. Springtime colours. Yet every minute she'd be forced to spend in this house would be harshest winter. As cold and unforgiving as the man who would ultimately claim her in that bed. She sat down on the edge of the bed and began to unfasten the trench coat. She was too tired to think any more and too angry to cry.

She dropped the rest of her clothes to the floor, and slid naked under the covers.

Persephone didn't have to stay in the Underworld, she

thought drowsily. But she ruined her chance to leave and go back to her old life when she succumbed to temptation and ate those pomegranate seeds.

But nothing and no one will ever distract me, she vowed grimly. Somehow, some day, I'm going to escape—and when I do, it will be for ever.

After three days, Joanna was reluctantly familiar with her new environment. She had begun by exploring the villa itself.

It was beautiful, with its wide marble floors and pale, un-adorned walls, but everything she saw seemed to confirm her initial impression that it was cold—even austere.

The main living room, or *saloni,* offered the most comfort, with a large fireplace, where logs were clearly burned during the winter months, fronted by a fur rug, and flanked by two massive cream leather sofas, deeply and luxuriously cushioned. The presence of a hi-fi system and a television set added a kind of normality, too, as did the glass-fronted bookcase crammed with titles in Greek, French and English.

Elsewhere, the furnishings, although elegant, had been kept to a minimum, and there were few ornaments, bowls of flowers or any of the individual touches that might give a hint of the owner's tastes. Yet this was his family home, so perhaps he was accustomed to this impersonal grandeur. But it seemed the last place where a man who sometimes looked like a pirate would come to relax.

There seemed no trace of him anywhere, she thought with faint bewilderment, nor, more tellingly, any mementoes of the woman who had been his wife.

Joanna looked in vain for a portrait on one of the walls, or even a photograph like the silver-framed picture of her mother that Denys always kept on the table beside his bed.

But perhaps Vassos Gordanis confined the poignant souvenirs of his marriage to his bedroom—the one place she had been careful to avoid.

And maybe, too, it wasn't the house, she thought, but the attitude of the staff which gave her such a sense of chill.

Because, she'd soon discovered, the men on the beach who'd ignored her had apparently established a precedent. There were, she'd learned from Stavros, over fifty people employed at the house, and in the olive groves and citrus orchards around it, most of whom lived on Thaliki and were ferried across on a daily basis.

But she rarely caught a glimpse of any of them, apart from Andonis, who served her meals with a kind of studied if monosyllabic courtesy, and of course Hara, who had radiated ungracious hostility from the first morning.

Although that did not prevent her from doing her job, Joanna admitted wryly. The hated mini-dress and other garments had been removed from the floor, never to return, while she slept. Her case had been unpacked, and its inadequate contents stowed in a mere fraction of the wardrobe space. And she was woken in grim silence each morning with coffee and the freshly laundered clothes from the day before.

Surely, she thought, if she had to be waited on, there must be someone younger and more cheerful among all these people.

But she soon discovered her mistake the first time she encountered one of the young maids upstairs and smiled, only to find the girl looking away and spitting three times.

When Joanna went to Stavros to express her indignation, he'd only shrugged. 'She cannot be blamed, *thespinis*. She was warding off the evil eye.'

'But that's ridiculous,' Joanna said hotly. 'There's no such thing.'

'Not in your country, perhaps. Here—is different. It is a strong belief,' he added drily. 'Be glad you do not have blue eyes.'

'Is that what they all think?' she demanded. 'That I'm some kind of witch?'

'*Ne, thespinis.* Having learned from Hara a little of the harm you have done, that is indeed what they believe.'

'From Hara?' Joanna drew a furious breath. 'Well, that settles it. Please find her something else to do. Because I don't want her hanging round me any more, like some—geriatric Medusa.'

'Hara is the sister of Andonis Leftanou, and she has served the Gordanis family faithfully for many years.' His eyes snapped at her. 'I advise you do not speak of her again without respect.' He paused ominously. 'If you know what is good for you.'

'Good for me?' Joanna echoed in derision. 'What in this whole ghastly situation could possibly be described as good for me?'

'You are fortunate that things have not been very much worse.'

'Oh, sure,' she threw back at him bitterly. 'And no doubt it's also an honour for me to be forced to *belong,* as you put it, to your disgusting employer. Well, I hope he rots in hell— and you with him!'

Stavros looked at her with distaste. 'I suggest you keep such thoughts to yourself, *thespinis.* Or when Kyrios Gordanis arrives here he may teach you a much-needed lesson,' he added grimly, and walked away.

In an attempt to keep occupied and fight her sense of isolation, she swam each day in the pool, then lay on the cushioned lounger under its parasol provided daily for her use by unseen hands. She ate her solitary though delicious meals, provided by Andonis' wife Penelope, in a vine-covered arbour at one end of the terrace, rested in her room with the shutters closed for an hour or so each afternoon and spent her evenings alone in the *saloni.*

She didn't dare touch the state-of-the-art music system, in spite of the mouth-watering record collection in its well-filled racks, and there were few English language programmes to tempt her on television. There was also a video machine,

with a number of pre-recorded cassettes, but these were la-
belled in Greek, and she wasn't sure how to operate the player
anyway.

And all hell would freeze before she asked for help of any
kind.

But if her days were difficult, the nights were far worse,
when she woke with a start from disturbing restless dreams,
convinced that a man's hand had stroked her face. Touched
her body. And that he was there, lying beside her, his skin hot
with desire.

Sometimes it was Peter Mansell who pressed his mouth
suffocatingly on hers as she tried to fight him away. But invariably the dream would change at some point, when her op-
pressor would become Vassos Gordanis, his ruthless kisses
stifling her pleas for help. Or for mercy.

It was all so terribly real. Too real. Because she awoke
each morning drained and on edge, a feeling of dread never
far from the pit of her stomach, wondering if this would be
the day when she would be made to pay for the past.

Knowing that this brief respite could not last, and that, for
her, time was running out.

CHAPTER SEVEN

JOANNA blew her nose vigorously, swallowing back the threatened tears. The last thing she wanted was someone to see her crying and misinterpret the reason, she thought, as she closed *Watership Down* and slipped the paperback into her bag together with her hankie.

During the past week, she'd devoured a Raymond Chandler and discovered Ernest Hemingway from the bookshelves in the *saloni,* but had hesitated to begin the book that Julie had given her, knowing that it would revive memories of the quiet evenings with baby Matthew—and a time when all she had to trouble her was shortage of money.

I didn't realise how lucky I was, she thought bitterly.

Suddenly restless, she got up from the lounger, putting on her hat and slinging her bag over her shoulder. Lunch would not be served for another hour or more, so she could fill in some time with a walk.

She'd explored most of the immediate vicinity, and all that remained was the unexciting prospect of the olive groves, where Stavros had assured her almost vehemently that there was nothing to see, and it would be better to go to the beach instead. He was probably right, she thought, but at least the trees would provide some shade, and less chance of running into an armed guard.

And it was pleasant to wander along, her espadrilles making no sound on the loose soil of the path winding between the trees, listening to the faint rustling of the silver leaves above her. There were nets spread on the ground beneath the branches, presumably to catch the fruit when it was harvested, in the way it had been done since the first olives were grown.

She recalled reading that the trees could live for hundreds of years, and, judging by the gnarled and twisted trunks she saw around her, some of these were very old indeed. Just being among them was an oddly peaceful experience.

And then she paused, frowning a little, as that peace was suddenly disturbed by the sound, not far away, of a child crying.

Except there were no children on the island. The only residents at the villa were Hara, who was a childless widow, and Andonis and Penelope, whose two sons were grown up and working on the mainland.

Puzzled, she followed the direction of the crying, and found herself on the edge of the grove, looking at a neat two-storey house fronted by its own fenced garden.

Yet Stavros had implied that the Villa Kore was the only house on the island.

And the house had occupants. A very small girl, incongruously clad in a pink taffeta dress, with a number of lace-edged underskirts, plus white shoes and socks, was standing at the gate, sobbing, her gaze fixed on a blue ball lying on the other side and well beyond her reach.

Joanna said gently, 'Oh, dear.' She picked up the ball and walked towards the gate, and saw the child retreat a couple of steps, her thumb in her mouth.

'Yours, I think.' Joanna pushed the ball carefully though the bars of the gate so that it bounced gently at the little girl's feet. 'And now you should say *efharisto*,' she prompted.

But the thumb stayed firmly and silently in place. Big dark eyes surveyed Joanna solemnly.

She was not, Joanna thought as she straightened, a very pretty child. But that was hardly her fault. Her black hair was pulled back into stiff braids, and the dress did nothing for her, either, being the wrong colour, and far too elaborate for playing in. What could her mother be thinking of?

She gave the little girl a swift, reassuring smile, then started back the way she'd come.

She heard a slight noise behind her and, turning, saw the ball was outside again, and the child back at the gate, watching hopefully. She said softly, 'So it's a game, is it?'

Retracing her steps, she returned the ball, but this time she only managed a couple of paces before she heard it bounce back again. She picked it up and walked to the gate, hunkering down so that she and the child were level.

Pointing to herself, she said, 'Joanna.'

But the child simply stared back unwinkingly and said nothing, her small face serious.

From inside the house, a female voice called sharply, 'Eleni,' and a young woman came out, shading her eyes from the sun. Olive-skinned and sloe-eyed, she had a full-lipped, sulky mouth, while a dark red dress made the most of a figure that bordered on the voluptuous.

As she caught sight of Joanna, her brows snapped together in a sharp frown and she marched down towards the gate, firing off a series of shrill questions in Greek.

'I'm sorry.' Joanna straightened awkwardly, passing the ball over the gate. 'I don't understand.'

The other halted, hands on hips, clearly taken aback. *'Anglitha?'*

Her voice sounded apprehensive, and when Joanna nodded, she crossed herself, seized the child's hand and began to tug her towards the house.

At the door, she turned. 'Go,' she said in halting, heavily accented English. 'You go. Not come here.'

More evil eye, I suppose, Joanna thought wearily as she retreated. But I only gave the poor little soul her ball back. I hardly turned her into a frog.

And you must have heard her crying, so why didn't you do something about it yourself?

Walking back to the villa, she kept picturing the small wistful face still looking back at her as she was being urged indoors by her mother. Besides the house being in the middle of nowhere, that garden was a very small playing space for a growing child, she thought, thinking of the expanse of unused lawn around the villa.

She recalled, too, one of her aunt's sayings—'all dressed up and nowhere to go.' Well, that was certainly true for little Eleni, she told herself with a pang.

As she emerged from the trees, a voice called, *'Thespinis,'* and she saw Stavros hurrying towards her, mopping his face with his handkerchief.

'I have been to the beach searching for you,' he told her snappishly. 'Where have you been?'

Joanna shrugged. 'Just for a walk,' she returned neutrally.

'You must come back to the house,' he said urgently. 'Come back quickly now. Because Kyrios Vassos is at Thaliki. Soon he will be here, and you must be waiting, *thespinis*. That is his order.'

All thoughts of quizzing him about her unexpected encounter vanished. Her heart was thudding unevenly.

She swallowed. 'He—he's on his way?'

'Have I not said so?' He gestured impatiently. 'Hara is waiting in your room. Make haste.'

The older woman swung round from the wardrobe as Joanna entered. She held up a dark green cotton skirt, ankle-length and patterned with daisies, and a scooped-neck blouse in broderie-anglaise.

'This,' she ordained brusquely. 'You wear this.' She paused. 'You wish bath or shower?'

Neither, with you around, Joanna thought. She said stonily, 'I can manage for myself—thank you.'

Hara gave her a beady look. 'You hurry. I return.'

Which was probably the longest verbal exchange they'd ever shared, Joanna thought.

Alone, she hung the skirt and top back in the wardrobe and

selected some white linen flared trousers and a matching shirt, covering her from throat to wrist.

The hall seemed full of people when she eventually descended the stairs, but they were all looking at the open door, where Andonis stood beaming, and not at her.

She sensed the excited stir, telling her the moment she'd dreaded had finally arrived. Then, as he walked in, clad only in ancient white shorts and a pair of canvas shoes, Joanna saw with a sudden lurch of the heart that the pirate had returned.

For an instant time spun away, and it was as if she was once more seeing him for the first time.

Except that she now realised what all those restless, troubled dreams had been telling her. That she knew exactly how that lean bronze body would feel against hers. How she would recognise the texture of his skin under her fingertips. And the taste of him beneath her lips.

He moved then, and she drew a hurried, horrified breath, her whole body taut as a bowstring, only to find him striding past her to where Hara was standing, and, in spite of her ample proportions, lifting her off her feet in a bear hug while she bridled in coy protest like a young girl, scolding fondly in Greek until he put her down.

Joanna thought helplessly that she had never seen such a change in anyone. Vinegar into honey. Never, surely, the same woman who, fifteen minutes ago, had thunderously condemned her choice of clothing as unsuitable attire in which to meet Kyrios Gordanis. And banged the door, muttering, when Joanna had refused point-blank to choose anything more feminine, or to loosen her hair, which she'd drawn severely back from her face and secured at the nape of her neck with a tortoiseshell clasp.

Hands clenched at her sides, she watched Vassos Gordanis greet Stavros, clapping him genially on the shoulder with a smiling word.

Then he turned to her, and all the laughter faded from his face, turning his mouth into a thin hard line.

For one absurd moment, she found herself thinking, no one will ever smile at me again…

Vassos Gordanis looked her over slowly, the harsh mockery in his eyes making her feel as if she'd been publicly stripped to the skin.

The clothes she had chosen covered her completely, just as she'd intended, but for one bewildered moment it was all she could do not to place protective hands in front of her body. Except that would amount to a victory for him, so she stood her ground, her own gaze defiant.

He said softly, 'Kyria Joanna—at last.' He paused. 'I trust you have not been too lonely without me.'

'Not at all,' she said. 'I hoped my solitude would never end.'

He shrugged. 'Who knows? You may find my company even more to your taste.'

She lifted her chin. 'Not in your lifetime, Mr Gordanis.'

'You sound very certain.' She heard the note of faint derision in his tone. 'But you may be persuaded to change your mind.' He paused, letting her know he'd absorbed her swift, angry intake of breath, then added flatly, 'Now, come and have lunch with me.'

'You do not seem very hungry.'

Joanna looked up from the grilled fish she was pushing round her plate. 'Are you surprised? When I'm being treated in this monstrous way?' She put down her fork. 'Please—why are you so determined to do this?'

'To make you pay in kind for what you did. But also…' he paused reflectively '…also for my private enjoyment. And I am no longer sure which is the more important consideration.'

She said rather breathlessly, 'Stick to your revenge, Mr Gordanis. You'll get nothing else from me.'

'There is a saying, I believe, that revenge is sweet.' His mouth curved cynically. 'Maybe you will demonstrate its truth.'

'You have no conscience, do you?' she said quietly, after a pause. 'No conscience at all.'

'And what of your own moral code, Joanna *mou?*' He poured himself some more wine. 'Which belongs, no doubt, to your country's much vaunted "permissive society".' He pronounced the phrase with scorn. 'Does that bear scrutiny, I wonder?'

Yes, she thought. *Yes!* Except in one instance that I have always regretted and that you have somehow discovered. And I never found Britain particularly permissive. Not with my aunt and uncle around.

'But this is a pointless discussion,' he went on. 'You are here with me because that is what I have decided, and you will remain also for as long as I decide. So accustom yourself, and quickly, because your protests do not impress me.'

His gaze flicked dismissively over her. 'Nor does this belated attempt at modesty,' he went on. 'You are for sale in a buyers' market, Joanna, and your charming body is your main asset,. I suggest you make the most of it later, when you are in bed with me.'

He added softly, 'When your only concealment, *agapi mou,* will be your beautiful hair.'

Joanna pressed her hands to her burning face. 'Don't.' She choked on the word. 'Oh, please—don't talk like that.'

'And you once dared to call me a hypocrite.' He sounded almost amused. 'So what would you prefer us to discuss?' He paused. 'Do you have a topic of interest? Or shall we speak instead of Petros Manassou?'

'I never knew anyone called that.' She didn't look at him, but knew her flush had deepened.

'Peter Mansell, then,' he said with a shrug. 'And do not pretend you have failed to make the connection. Honesty will serve you better now.'

She bit her lip. 'Perhaps—but I don't understand what he has to do with you.'

He said flatly, 'He is the only son of my cousin Maria. Does that make the situation clearer for you?'

Her heart sank like a stone. *Oh, God—oh, God...*

'Yes—I suppose,' she said at last. 'But why was he using a different name?'

'He went to Australia to carry out a business transaction, for the first time unsupervised. He wished, it seems, to prove himself.' His mouth tightened. 'To demonstrate he could succeed in this without reference to his family connections.'

By bragging everywhere about his money? Crowing over his commercial acumen? All the deals he'd achieved single-handed?

She kept her head bent. 'You thought he was old enough—experienced enough—to be trusted?'

'I knew nothing of it until it was too late,' he answered coldly. 'He was sent by his future father-in-law, apparently to test his ambition and his reliability. Without your intervention he might possibly have done so. Fortunately the money your dubious friends took from him formed only the first tranche in a complicated series of payments. But it was enough to ruin him and the future he'd hoped for.'

'You said his future father-in-law.' Joanna swallowed. 'He was—going to be—married?'

Peter had never even hinted at that, she thought. On the contrary, he'd boasted openly about his bachelor status. Given the impression that all the girls in California were at his feet.

And all of it complete and utter fantasy.

'Once,' he said. 'No longer, however. Maybe never—until his criminal folly can be forgotten. I arranged for the money to be repaid, of course, but after such a betrayal of trust the bride's family broke off the engagement, and made no secret of their reasons. It has caused a breach between friends that may never heal.' He paused. 'Yet, fortunately for his ex-fiancée, who is a pious, modest girl and Maria's goddaughter, they only know half the story. Your part in it Petros confessed to me alone. Not even his mother knows of his shame in that respect.

She has experienced enough heartbreak over this whole affair, so she was told only that I would pursue and punish the gamblers who cheated him.'

He added softly, 'And I have done so. You, Joanna *mou,* are the last. And in your case I decided, as they say, that your punishment should fit your crime. Exactly.'

She touched her tongue to her dry lips. 'And everyone knows this—of course? Even—Hara?'

'Especially Hara,' he said harshly. 'She was my nanny when I was a baby, then went to my cousin when Petros was born.' The dark gaze was scornful. 'It is as if you had harmed her own child.'

A perfect child who naturally could not be blamed for his youthful mistakes. And who had, anyway, found his own scapegoat.

'Please,' she said huskily. 'Please—you must let me explain…'

'No explanation is necessary,' he denied brusquely. 'Petros is young and still naïve about women, which must have made it pitifully easy for you to become his pillow friend—show him what he thought was Paradise—then lead him to your associates like an Easter lamb to the butcher's knife.'

Joanna said hoarsely. 'He said that? That I'd— That we'd…' She was nearly choking. 'But he can't have done. Because it isn't true—I swear it. Oh, God, you—you have to believe me.'

'No,' he said. 'I do not. Or do you think I share the naïveté of my fool of a cousin? You forget, Joanna *mou,* I watched you that night in France, and so did every other man present, wondering what it would be like to have you under him—to touch you and kiss—to possess you. Just as you intended. And as you did to that boy.'

He lit a cheroot and drew on it, watching her through the smoke. 'Petros assures me your performance in private is an even greater thrill than the public display,' he added almost casually. 'That, in bed, you are inventive and inexhaustible as well as beautiful. Let us hope his judgement does not err—in this at least.'

How could he have said that? Joanna wondered dazedly, cringing from the memory of Peter Mansell's hoarse breathing, the unavailing attempts to push his tongue into her mouth. The hands pawing clumsily at her breasts while she fought to hide her revulsion.

But the fact that he'd lied about her so hideously—gone to such appalling lengths to justify his conduct—did not make her guiltless, although she would have given anything in the world to be able to throw the entire accusation back in Vassos Gordanis' mocking face.

To tell him passionately that she'd done nothing—*nothing*. That Peter/Petros was a coward and an idiot, totally and stupidly responsible for the troubles his own conceit had brought on him.

Except, of course, she couldn't say that. Because she had indeed let him suppose that she might belong to him—eventually. And she could also have stopped him going to the poker game. Could have warned him off somehow, then made up some story to account for his absence, braving the wrath of Diamond Lenny.

But she had not. Leaving her, she realised wretchedly, with no real defence. And facing instead the wrath of Vassos Gordanis.

'Your silence is revealing, *pedhi mou*,' he commented. He got to his feet and walked round the table, pulling her up from her chair and holding her against him, creating a moment when she was aware of the warmth of his bare chest penetrating the thin fabric of her shirt and felt her nipples harden suddenly against the lacy confinement of her bra.

She smothered a gasp of pure shock and lifted her hands, pushing him away and taking a swift instinctive step backwards.

His mouth twisted cynically. 'However, it seems our time apart has not yet endeared me to you, Joanna *mou*,' he remarked. 'But be warned. I find your attitude a challenge, not a deterrent. If you fight me you will lose, and the manner of my victory may not be to your taste. Do you understand me?'

It would be truthful to say no. To explain that nothing in her life had prepared her for this. For him. But knew that he would not believe her.

'Yes.' Her voice was barely a whisper. 'I—understand...'

Vassos Gordanis nodded abruptly. 'And now there are matters that demand my attention so I must tear myself away from you.' He took her hand and raised it, brushing her clenched knuckles with his lips. It was the briefest caress but it seemed to shiver through her entire being, increasing this whole new dimension of physical awareness that had come so shockingly into being when she'd found herself in his arms.

Leaving her mute and trembling when he released her.

'But only, I promise, for a little while,' he added mockingly, and went.

I can't stay here just—waiting, Joanna thought desperately, watching his tall figure walk back into the villa. *I can't...*

She looked down at her fingers as if expecting to see them branded by the touch of his mouth.

Because she deserved to be marked, she told herself with bitterness. She should carry a lasting scar for that instant of supreme folly—supreme weakness.

How could such fleeting contact evoke a physical response she had never dreamed could exist—or imagined she would ever be capable of? Especially with him.

She felt almost sick with self-betrayal.

But at least he doesn't know, she thought desperately. And I must make certain that he never finds out.

So she couldn't go on standing there in the sunlight as if she'd been turned to stone like the statue of Persephone. She had to try and hide her inner turmoil, and behave as if this was any other day. And that Vassos Gordanis' arrival had prompted nothing but her indifference.

Act like the girl he thinks I am, she told herself. Uncaring and unprincipled.

Tension was building in her, like a knotted cord twisted round her forehead. She lifted a hand to release the clip fastening her hair, then paused as she remembered his words—*your only concealment...*

And shivered at the thought of what awaited her that night.

Although there was nothing she could do. This was his house. His island. If she ran away and hid somewhere, she'd simply be found and brought back to face his displeasure.

And in some strange way the thought of his anger was almost worse than the prospect of the other kind of passion she could expect from him.

There was only one place for her to go. The room that had been almost a refuge since she arrived. That might still provide her with sanctuary if only for a few hours. Until Vassos Gordanis had completed his work and remembered her again.

Slowly, head bent, she walked into the house and went upstairs.

As she walked into the bedroom she halted, thinking she'd come to the wrong place. Because it was like a warehouse, the floor and bed strewn with flat beribboned boxes and crumpled tissue paper. And in the middle of it all Hara, directing two of the maids who were hanging things in the wardrobe and placing them in the drawers.

Dresses, Joanna saw with disbelief, and skirts in silk and lawn. Soft floating things. Filmy nightgowns and negligees. Lace underwear.

She said, 'What is this?'

'Clothes, *thespinis,* for you to wear.' Hara didn't add, For the pleasure of Kyrios Gordanis, because she didn't have to. As the furtive exchange of glances between the maids made more than clear.

A rich man was indulging his mistress, who would be

expected to show him proper gratitude for his generosity when they were alone. Or not…

Joanna lifted her chin. 'Then you can just take them away,' she said crisply. 'Because I don't want them.'

'This is the order of the *kyrie*.' Hara's tone was firm. 'He is not to be disobeyed.'

Joanna picked up the two nearest boxes, walked to the open window and out on to the little balcony, and threw them over its rail.

'And unless you obey *me,* the rest will go the same way,' she informed her gaping audience. 'I have clothes and I require nothing from Kyrios Gordanis. So get it all out of here and then go, please. I have a headache.'

There was a horrified silence, then Hara said something curt in her own language and the two girls began removing the garments and carrying them away in armfuls, whispering together as they did so.

When it was finished, and the maids had gone, Hara said quietly, 'This is not wise, *thespinis*.'

'Really?' Joanna met her gaze defiantly. 'Well, I don't think I care any more.'

Hara went on looking at her, but an odd bewilderment had replaced her usual hostility, and something that was almost pity.

Although that was nonsense. Hara might not wholly approve of the way her master was conducting his revenge, but at the same time she was a Greek woman who probably believed in Nemesis, the goddess of retribution. She would no doubt think that Joanna had asked for all the trouble that was coming her way and then some. There was no sisterhood here.

She said, 'You wish I get you something—for the headache?'

'No,' Joanna returned. 'I just want to be alone—please.'

There was another silence, then Hara shrugged and left, closing the door quietly behind her.

Joanna sat down on the edge of the bed, running a weary

hand round the nape of her neck. She felt hot and sticky, and the thought of a cool shower had a definite appeal.

Collecting her elderly white cotton dressing gown, she trailed into the bathroom and set the water running, before discarding her clothes and pinning her hair on top of her head.

The gentle cascade was like balm against her heated skin as she soaped her body, then rinsed and rinsed again.

As she patted herself dry she gave a small sigh of satisfaction, then reached for her robe, tying the sash loosely round her slender waist.

She unfastened her hair and shook it loose as she walked back into the bedroom.

And stopped dead in her tracks, her eyes dilating.

'You have been a long time, *matia mou,*' said Vassos Gordanis. He too was wearing a robe, but in crimson silk, as he lounged on the bed. 'I began to think I would have to fetch you.'

He smiled at her. 'But here you are—so my waiting is over at last. Now, come to me.'

CHAPTER EIGHT

For a moment Joanna stood staring at him, unable to move or speak. Those last few precious hours of freedom she'd counted were gone, she realised dazedly. Time had finally run out.

Eventually, she said hoarsely, 'I—I don't understand. I thought—you—you said you had work to do.'

He shrugged, the robe slipping away from one tanned, muscular shoulder. 'I found concentration difficult, *agapi mou*. During our separation I found that I desired you more than I had planned to do. So I decided that while work could wait, you could not. And I could not.' He held out his hand. '*Ela etho,*' he commanded softly. 'Come here.'

She said, dry-mouthed, 'It's the middle of the afternoon!'

'The time of siesta,' he said. 'A habit I understand you have acquired since your arrival. Today you will spend it with me instead of alone.'

'But I have a headache.' She despised herself for the note of pleading she could hear in her voice.

'I also ache,' he said with faint amusement. 'But in a different way. Perhaps we will heal each other.' He added more crisply, 'And now, Joanna *mou,* please do not weary me with any further excuses. You know why you are here.'

She made herself move then. Made herself walk to the bed, knowing with certainty that there was nothing else she could do, and also that there was a part of her—a part she tried desperately to banish—that flared with sparks of excitement.

He took her hand, drawing her down beside him not ungently. She saw that he was no longer smiling. Instead his expression was serious—even intense—as he reached for the sash of her robe and untied it slowly, almost carefully, pushing apart its concealing folds.

She knew that this was only the beginning, but all the same she turned her head away, closing her eyes so she would not have to see his dark gaze burning over her naked body.

If I don't look at him, she thought, maybe I can pretend this isn't really happening. But that won't work, either, because he's been there in my dreams every night since we first met. Which is something I need to forget.

The silence that followed was broken only by his sigh of pleasure, hardly more than a breath.

She lay still as he removed her robe completely, her hands clenched at her sides to hide the fact that her body was, against her will, responding to his touch.

He said softly, 'You are very lovely. But worth the ruin of a man's whole future life? I truly wonder.'

She had not, of course, realised that shutting off the sight of him would simply heighten all her other senses, making her vividly aware of the slight dip in the mattress as he moved even closer. So close that she thought she could feel the strong heavy beat of his heart echo in her own bloodstream. Could absorb the clean, soap-enhanced scent of his warm skin. Hear the sharp rustle of silk as he discarded his own robe.

He began to touch her, his hand skimming lightly from the curve of her cheek down her throat to her shoulder, then moulding the slender outline of her body in one long, sweeping movement that, in spite of her inexperience, Joanna recognised as more a declaration of intent than a caress. A gesture that promised total possession.

In her self-imposed darkness, she was conscious of other things, too. The strange sensation of a man lying next to her, his heated nakedness grazing her own skin. The powerful and potent reality of his male arousal.

She felt his fingers cup her chin, turning her face towards him, and then experienced the first brush of his lips on hers, lingering, searing, and oddly, unexpectedly gentle. He kissed her again, his mouth persuasive—insistent. Seeking, some instinct told her, the beginnings of a surrender she dared not risk. Because once she had yielded she knew with utter certainty that there would be no way back—and, more shockingly, nor did she want there to be.

His hand found her small breast, taking its rounded softness in his palm, his thumb teasing her nipple and bringing it to aching, hardening life with an ease that amazed her. And warned her, too, that her lips were beginning to soften under the subtle pressure of his kiss. Even—parting…

With a gasp, she jerked her mouth from his, at the same time seizing his wrist and dragging it away from her.

She felt him pause, and waited, her pulses pounding unevenly. Wondering.

He said quietly, 'Look at me.'

She obeyed unwillingly, her gaze uncertain as it met his.

'So what are you telling me, *matia mou?*' Propped on an elbow, he studied her, his expression enigmatic. 'That any further attempt to arouse you for our mutual pleasure would be wasted?'

No, she thought. That I'm out of my depth and liable to drown in a sea of longing. Because you make me feel—make me want impossible things. And I can't let that happen. I can't let *you* happen.

'Think what you please.' She found a voice from somewhere, as she stared rigidly past him. 'It makes no odds to me. I hate and despise you, Vassos Gordanis, and nothing you say or do to me will change that. Not now. Not ever.'

There was a tingling silence, then Vassos said softly, 'If you imagine I shall appreciate such frankness you are wrong. My own wishes are very different.' His hand cupped her chin as he stared down at her, his dark eyes brooding. 'But I am not unrealistic. I expect you to give no more than you have offered in the past to any other man.'

She swallowed. 'I offer nothing, Kyrios Gordanis. So—take what you want, then leave me alone.'

'And if I had met you under other circumstances, is that still what you would have said to me?' He moved, drawing her closer. 'If I had come ashore from *Persephone* that afternoon and found you, asked you to come with me—be with me— would you have fought me then?'

'Yes,' she said, aware that her heart was suddenly thudding against her ribcage. 'Because once you'd discovered who I was you'd have remembered your revenge, and everything would have been just the same.'

'Perhaps,' he said. 'But—I wonder. About that—and also other things.' He bent his head, brushing her mouth once more with his, surprising her with his sudden gentleness. 'For example,' he went on softly, 'how can lips that speak such hard words taste so sweet?'

The erratic behaviour of her heartbeat held her mute as, once more, his fingertips stroked her breast, luring the delicate nipple to pucker in response before taking it between his lips in an arousal as delicious as it was irresistible.

Only she had to resist it, she thought, stifling a gasp. That— and the slow, beguiling glide of his hand down her flushed and restless body to the curve of her hip. Had to, or she would never be able to live with the shame of it.

Vassos raised his head and looked down at her. He said quietly, 'I warned you that I would not be cheated of my satisfaction, and I meant it. But it is a pleasure I find that I wish you to share, Joanna *mou*. So—I ask you to put your arms around me and give me your lovely mouth.'

She said huskily, 'You ask for too much.'

A bronzed shoulder lifted in a shrug. 'Then remember, *matia mou,* that the choice was yours.'

He lifted himself over her, almost negligently parting her

thighs with his knee, before sliding his hands under her flanks and lifting her towards him.

Joanna felt the rigid hardness of him pressing against her, demanding entry to the secret place of her womanhood, and gave in to the sudden scald of excitement deep within her.

Hastily, she shut her eyes again, telling herself it was so that she would not have to see his smile of triumph as he achieved his ultimate revenge. Knowing that she had to hide that unwelcome, impossible stir of desire in case he recognised it. Determined to deny him any kind of response, whatever the cost.

Vassos moved with commanding purpose, penetrating her with one powerful thrust of his loins, and in that same instant her world blurred into a pain she'd never dreamed could exist as her virgin flesh impeded his invasion.

Spikes of coloured light danced behind her closed lids, her resolution to remain silent and passive forgotten with her first shocked cry.

Then, it was over. She heard him say, *'Theos,'* his voice raw and shaken, then pull away from her. Out of her.

Vassos flung himself on his back beside her, his breathing hoarse and ragged, and she lay motionless, slow tears squeezing from beneath her lids and scalding a path down her face. The flash of pain had subsided, and his withdrawal had left her hating herself for aching for his continued touch.

He moved again, and Joanna flinched involuntarily. But he was only reaching for his robe and dragging it on, fastening the belt as he left the bed and walked to the door. He threw it wide and shouted an imperative summons.

A moment later Hara appeared, and he bent his head, talking softly and rapidly in his own language. Joanna saw the older woman's hand go to her cheek in a kind of horror as she listened. She began to speak, but he silenced her, patting her shoulder and turning her towards the bed before he left, closing the door quietly behind him.

Which, in some strange way, seemed to make things a

hundred times worse, Joanna thought numbly. Simply watching him walk away, without a word except a muttered blasphemy.

A sob rose in her throat, and then another, and she found she was crying in earnest, her body shaking as she turned to bury her wet face in the pillow.

And then she felt herself lifted with astonishing gentleness and held against Hara's generous bosom, while her hair was stroked and words were murmured that she could not comprehend but which sounded oddly comforting just the same.

She didn't understand this *volte face,* but somehow it didn't seem to matter.

It was a while before she felt sufficiently in command of herself to draw back, wiping her wet face with her fingers.

She saw Hara looking down at the bed, and, following her gaze, saw with desperate embarrassment that there was blood on her thighs and on the sheet.

She said shakily, 'Oh, God—I—I'm so sorry.'

'No need for sorrow.' Hara's tone was kind but firm. 'Sometimes, for a girl, the first time is easy. For others, like you, not good. It is how it is.' She touched Joanna's hot cheek. 'And now that Kyrios Vassos knows that you are a girl of purity—of honour—he will be kind to you in bed. Make sure there is no more pain, only pleasure.' She smiled. 'Now I fill bath for you.'

'No,' Joanna said. 'That's the last thing I want.'

'Not bath?' Hara was bewildered.

'Mr Gordanis being—kind.' She sat up. 'He'll never come near me—never touch me again.'

'*Po, po, po.* Such foolishness,' Hara chided. 'How could he know? If he had been husband on wedding night, same pain, same blood.' She gave Joanna a look that was almost roguish. 'There will be more loving. You are beautiful girl, Kyria Joanna. You need beautiful man to give you joy in bed. Make…' She stopped suddenly, an awkward expression flitting across her face. 'Make much happiness.'

And she bustled off to the bathroom, leaving Joanna to wonder what she'd intended to say.

But, she discovered, she was glad of the bath. Thankful to sink down into warm scented water and reclaim her body.

If only, she thought, it was as easy to erase from her mind the way her body had reacted to his touch at the beginning—how her lips had bloomed under his kiss and her breast had seemed to swell under the provocative stroke of his fingers.

The way her body had seemed prepared to welcome him.

And, to her eternal shame, she felt her nipples again tauten into rosebuds at the memory.

There was more humiliation waiting for her in the bedroom. The maids who'd been there earlier were just leaving, having changed the bedlinen at Hara's direction.

Now everyone in the house would know what had happened, she thought, and wanted to howl all over again.

Hara sat her on the dressing stool and began to brush her hair.

'You rest now,' she ordained. 'Later, I bring the new dresses,' she added guilelessly. 'Make you look beautiful for Kyrios Vassos.'

'No,' Joanna said, swiftly and definitely. 'I meant what I said. I won't accept anything he's bought me. And I don't want to look beautiful for anyone—least of all him. Because if I'd been ugly I wouldn't be here, and none of this would have happened.'

Argue with that, she thought, but Hara didn't even try. She simply closed the shutters, drew the curtains, and put Joanna to bed as if she was a child, covering her with a sheet.

'Now sleep, *pedhi mou*,' she said quietly, and went.

But oblivion, so much desired, was a long time coming. Joanna was too tense, too alert, every distant quiet noise of an occupied house assailing her ears in stereophonic sound, and her eyes constantly returning to the door, scared that it would open to admit him.

Because how could she ever bear to face him again—even if he didn't want—want…?

But there was no question of that, she assured herself. He would let her go now. He had to. She'd surely paid for what she'd done, so there was no reason for him to keep her any longer. Not when she would never provide him with the kind of entertainment he required.

She burrowed deeper into the mattress, shivering. How could she have allowed herself to be used like that? She would make sure that no man ever got close enough again to treat her in the same way. She would rather remain celibate for the rest of her life.

She slept at last, deeply and dreamlessly, and woke to find vivid sunset light falling in slats across the floor.

For a moment she wanted to stay where she was. To ask for her dinner to be served up here in this room. Except he might join her, and she could not risk that.

Behave as this was any other evening, she thought, gritting her teeth as she pushed the sheet back. As if nothing had happened between you. Or nothing that mattered anyway.

She washed and cleaned her teeth, then swept back her hair and plaited it into one long braid before dressing in the daisy skirt and cotton top she'd rejected only that morning, and not the lifetime ago that it seemed.

As she descended the wide sweep of marble stair, she looked across at the statue of Persephone.

You should never have eaten those pomegranate seeds, she thought. But I won't make the same mistake, because I'll accept nothing from Vassos Gordanis. Not one stitch of clothing, not one stone of jewellery. And none of this so-called 'kindness,' because I know what that really means.

And I'll give nothing, either. Not a kiss, a touch nor a smile of my own free will—no matter what he does. I'll make him desperate to be rid of me.

'Thespinis.' She realised with a start that Stavros had appeared, and was waiting for her at the foot of the stairs. 'Kyrios Vassos wishes to speak with you in his study.'

How totally incongruous that sounded, she thought, as she nodded briefly and followed him. As if she was being summoned to the school principal's office for a reprimand.

She was taken to a room at the rear of the house, overlooking the swimming pool.

Vassos was sitting at a massive desk, checking a sheaf of papers in front of him. As Joanna entered he put down his pen and rose to his feet. He was wearing white jeans that hugged his lean hips, topped by a dark red shirt, open nearly to the waist.

It was almost the same colour as the robe he'd worn earlier, and for a moment she paused, her memories holding her captive.

Don't let him see, she repeated silently. Don't let him see…

'Kalispera.' His voice was coolly courteous, as if, for him, those brief tumultuous moments in her bedroom had never happened. 'Please have a chair.'

Not a rebuke after all, she told herself, a bubble of hysteria building inside her as she seated herself opposite him. But something that seemed more like a job interview.

He opened a drawer in the desk and extracted the UK passport which had been taken from her by Stavros before she left France. He flicked it open, studied her photograph, then skimmed through the other pages. He put it down and looked at her.

He said quietly, 'Joanna Vernon. So you are related to him, and never his mistress as you appeared to be.' He paused. 'Levaux told me there was a story that you were his niece, which no one believed. Is it perhaps true?'

Joanna hesitated, then shook her head, realising that there was little point in persisting with the fabrication. She said, 'Not his niece. His—his daughter.'

'Daughter?' The word was almost explosive. He leaned

forward, resting clenched fists on the desk, the dark eyes blazing. 'You say you are his *daughter?* Is he quite mad? What kind of father is he to treat his own child in such a way—expose her to such dangers? Such shame?'

She smoothed a non-existent crease from her skirt. 'Perhaps a desperate one.'

'That is an excuse?'

'No,' she said. 'A reason, but not one that a man with your money could ever understand.'

'You are wrong,' he bit back at her. 'Wealth does not make one immune from desperation or any other condition of the human spirit.' He shook his head. 'And your mother permitted him to do this? How is it possible?'

'No.' There were tears thick in her throat, and she swallowed them back. 'I started travelling with Daddy after my mother died. He said he—needed me.'

He muttered something harsh and ugly under his breath, then sat down, glancing at the passport again. 'You are—eighteen?'

'Almost nineteen.'

'A child still.'

'Hardly that,' she said. 'Any longer.'

His mouth tightened. Then, 'A child,' he repeated coldly. 'Whose innocence he chose to barter. It is beyond belief. Beyond decency. How could he do such a thing?'

'He is a gambler,' Joanna said slowly. 'He was on a winning streak, and facing the opportunity of a lifetime. It probably didn't occur to him that he could lose. It rarely did, even when he could afford to do so.' She paused. 'And of course he didn't know how heavily the odds were stacked against him.'

He said softly, 'That final hand. You think perhaps I cheated? I did not.'

'What does it matter—now? What does anything matter?' She lifted her head and looked at him. 'And who are you to dare talk of decency? If you'd had even a streak of humanity you wouldn't have enforced that bet. No one could possibly sink that low.'

He said slowly, 'Petros lied when he said you had given him your body, but did he lie about the rest? Did you lure him to be cheated at that card game?'

'Yes.' She bit her lip. 'He—he told you the truth about that.'

'And was it your own idea or the suggestion of your father that you should do this?'

Joanna swallowed. 'Not—just him.'

'Then your answer is yes, and he deserved to be punished in the way I had chosen,' he said flatly. 'Even though I thought I was taking his pillow friend, not his daughter.'

'And if you'd known?' she said. 'If he'd told you—appealed to you—would it have made any difference?'

There was a silence, then he said, 'No, Joanna *mou,* on re-flection—it would not. On the contrary, it would have taken my revenge on him to another dimension—to watch him real-ise exactly what he had lost and suffer.'

She said breathlessly, 'You think he isn't suffering now—knowing the hell he's condemned me to and unable to help me?'

'If so, he is being tortured in comfort, Joanna *mou,* as you are yourself.' His mouth curled. 'It seems your father left France in the company of a Mrs Van Dyne. I am told she is a rich New York socialite.'

She stared at him.

'I don't believe you,' she said at last, her voice uneven. 'If it was true—if he's all right—why hasn't he come to find me?'

Vassos shrugged. 'Perhaps because he would have to reveal your true relationship to his new companion, and it is not con-venient for him to do so at this time.' His glance was measur-ing. 'Would you have told me of it if you were still a virgin? I think not.'

She stared down at her hands, tightly clasped in her lap.

'Well, now you've punished us both, and your revenge is complete. So you don't need to keep me any longer.'

'Our views of necessity differ, Joanna *mou*. And I have no intention of allowing you to leave,' he added softly. 'At least not until I have had everything I want from you. And how long that will take, only you can decide.'

She said huskily, 'I—I don't know what you mean.'

'Begin thinking like a woman,' he said, 'and it will soon become clear. Which brings me to something I must ask you. May I assume that your total lack of experience extends also to the use of birth control? You do not have to speak,' he added as embarrassed colour stormed into her face. 'Just nod or shake your head.'

He watched the tiny movement of confirmation, and sighed. 'As I thought,' he commented, half to himself. 'And does it also follow that you have no wish to bear me a child?'

She looked up quickly, her eyes blank with horror as she met his frankly sardonic gaze.

'Again I have my answer,' he murmured. 'So I shall take the responsibility for your protection. When, of course, your body has had time to recover from its recent ordeal,' he added courteously.

She said hoarsely, 'Am I expected to thank you?'

He shrugged. 'Perhaps, one day, you may be grateful.' He got to his feet. 'And now I must return to the tasks I neglected earlier. We will meet again at dinner, Joanna *mou*.' He paused. 'When you will choose something to wear from the clothes I have brought you. They have all been returned to your room— even those you threw in the garden.'

She rose, too, and faced him, lifting her chin. 'I would prefer not to.'

'But it is not your preference that is under consideration,' he said. 'And if you continue to defy me I shall dress you with my own hands.' His smile grazed her. 'It will be no hardship, believe me. The reality of you naked exceeded anything I had imagined.'

He watched the heated colour swamp her face, his smile widening.

'And to know that I will be the first to enjoy you completely is an undreamed of pleasure also,' he told her softly. 'I look forward to the moment.'

He sat down, reaching for the papers he'd been reading earlier.

'Until later, then,' he added, as Joanna turned and headed blindly for the door

CHAPTER NINE

Joanna felt drained when she reached her bedroom that night. She had it to herself, to her relief, although Hara had clearly been there at some point, to turn the bed down on one side only.

She changed into one of her own cotton nightshirts, hanging the slender shift in leaf-green silk that she'd worn for dinner back in the wardrobe with the rest of the clothing Vassos Gordanis had provided, then sat down to brush her hair.

This must rank, she thought, as the worst evening she'd ever spent—in the company of a man who had deliberately outraged her both physically and emotionally, and announced his intention of continuing to do so at some future point.

An abnormal, even impossible situation by any standard, which he, somehow, had made seem almost normal and even—feasible.

Because when he eventually joined her in the *saloni* he had turned into the perfect host, politely attentive and, she thought, grinding her teeth in chagrin, undeniably charming.

He had acknowledged the new dress with a slight inclination of the head, but there'd been none of the edged remarks she'd expected.

He'd offered her ouzo, which she'd refused, and white wine which, against her better judgement, he'd persuaded her to accept.

And then, over a lamplit dinner on the terrace, he'd chatted to her, lightly and without any hint of flirtation, let alone sexual innuendo, on neutral topics, and in a way that demanded a response from her that could not be as exclusively monosyllabic as she'd planned.

Someone had clearly told him she was a reader, because he enquired as to her favourite authors. Whether she preferred Dickens to Thomas Hardy, or *Jane Eyre* to *Wuthering Heights*. Asked if she'd enjoyed *The Day of the Jackal* and if she thought *The Dogs of War* was as good.

'You must tell me if there are any books you would like to read, and I will get them for you,' he went on, and Joanna looked away.

More pomegranate seeds, she thought, but she was not going to be tempted.

However, it was a novelty for her to have this kind of conversation again. Denys had no interest in books, and had often told her she was wasting time reading when she could have been acquiring skills as a poker player which would stand her in good stead for the future.

It occurred to her, reluctantly, that if Vassos Gordanis had been anyone else she might almost have begun to enjoy herself. And realised just how dangerous that was.

'But it seems you do not care for music,' he said, over the coffee that had been served indoors in the *saloni*.

'That's not true,' Joanna said defensively. 'I'm just not used to that kind of system.'

'Ah,' he said. 'You wish me to demonstrate its use, perhaps?'

'No, thank you. It—it's not important.' She put down her empty cup and drew a breath. 'May I go to my room, please?'

He glanced in surprise at his watch. 'So early? Why?'

'Because I—I can't do this,' she said raggedly. 'Can't sit here and chat as if—as if…'

'As if we were friends?' he supplied with a touch of mockery. 'You don't think in time we may become so?'

'I know we won't.'

'You disappoint me,' he said softly. 'However, run away, if that is what you wish.'

She was on her way to the door but she halted, swinging round to confront him.

'Wish?' she repeated. 'Do you know what I really wish, Mr Gordanis?'

'Of course, Joanna *mou*,' he drawled. 'You would like never to set eyes on me again, unless I am lying dead at your feet. Is that a summary of your feelings?'

'Yes,' she said defiantly.

'But sadly your wish will not be gratified, unlike my own.' He paused. 'And my name is Vassos,' he added. 'In future you will use it, if you please.'

'I take it,' she said, 'that is an order, not an option?'

'Bravo, *pedhi mou*.' His smile mocked her. 'You are beginning to learn.'

And today's lesson would seem to be don't challenge him, Joanna thought, as she put down her hairbrush and rose. Just put up and shut up.

It was a hot still night, and she opened her balcony doors to catch any stray breath of wind before fastening the shutters.

She turned back the coverlet, folding it neatly at the foot of the bed, then slipped under the sheet. As she turned to switch off the bedside lamp she heard the rattle of a door handle, and Vassos sauntered into the room.

He was barefoot, wearing black silk pyjama pants that sat low on his lean hips.

Joanna involuntarily pulled the sheet tighter, her eyes dilating as he walked towards the bed.

He halted, brows lifting as he regarded her. 'You have nothing to fear tonight, *pedhi mou*, I give you my word. But I did not bring you to this house in order to sleep alone. Although I have decided for once to spare your blushes,' he added, indicating his attire, his tone almost rueful. 'In truth I had forgotten I possessed such things.'

He turned off the light and slid into bed beside her, reaching for her and drawing her quivering body against his in one easy movement.

'Relax,' he told her softly as she tried to pull away, bracing a hand against his shoulder. 'I ask only that you lie quietly in my arms. Accustom yourself to being in bed with me.'

She said hoarsely, her heart hammering as she experienced the warmth of him against her, penetrating the thin cotton of her nightshirt, 'Never. Never in this world.'

'But this is a different world, Joanna *mou*.' He took her hand from his shoulder, placing it instead on his hair-roughened chest, so that the heavy beat of his heart resonated through her palm. His other arm went round her, holding her, his fingers resting lightly on her hip. 'A world where your life is mine,' he added quietly. 'So try to accept that. And me.'

She felt the fleeting pressure of his lips on her hair. 'Now, let us sleep.'

Sleep? her mind screamed silently. No matter how tired she was, did he really think she could simply curl up against him and close her eyes? Was he mad?

She lay, staring up at the ceiling, silently counting the minutes, listening—waiting on tenterhooks for his breathing to deepen—to become rhythmic. For his clasp to slacken.

Eventually, when she thought enough time had passed and it seemed safe, she began to move, trying to edge slowly and carefully away from him. But, to her exasperation, her progress was minimal, hampered by the soft mattress and the cling of the sheet.

While reclaiming her hand from his chest was yet another problem. As she tried to slide her fingers out from beneath his, she found herself encountering far too much warm, bare skin.

Frustrated, she made a final determined attempt to lift herself away, only to feel her knee graze his silk-clad thigh.

As she froze, his voice came to her in the darkness, his tone even, almost conversational. 'Continue to wriggle like that if you wish, *pedhi mou,* but I should warn you my self-control is not limitless.' He paused. 'However, you might be more comfortable like this.'

He turned on to his side and pulled her back against him, wrapping his arms round her, and shaping her to the curve of his body.

He whispered, 'Now, close your eyes.'

Burning with helpless resentment, she obeyed, although she knew she still wouldn't be able to sleep. Not—close to him like this.

For one thing, she couldn't empty her mind of images from the past twenty-four hours. And not just the memory of what had happened in this bed a few hours earlier.

It was the other aspects of him that were teasing at her brain, from the laughing pirate who'd come striding in to recapture his domain, to the cold-eyed interrogator who'd faced her across his desk, demanding truths that had come too late to save her, who'd then in some extraordinary way become a pleasant companion at dinner.

And, strangest of all, the man who was holding her at this moment, quietly and without threat, his steady breath warm on her neck. A situation she didn't really wish to contemplate.

Yet Vassos Gordanis was not the only enigma that Pellas had to offer, she thought. And it was much safer to think about the other one.

To contemplate the house in the olive grove, and remember a small child dressed up for a non-existent party who'd briefly enjoyed a simple, silly game, as well as the shrill voice of the mother who'd warned her to stay away.

But why? she wondered. What harm had it done to befriend a little girl who'd seemed to share her own sense of isolation?

Besides, what was that kind of sultry beauty doing in the back of beyond? Unless, like a good wife, she lived where her husband's work took her.

Except, of course, the Gordanis workforce lived on Thaliki, so why was this little family an apparent exception?

But I can't think about that now, Joanna decided drowsily. I'll mention it to Hara. I'll do that tomorrow after I've had my swim. The one good thing about being here.

She imagined herself in the pool, floating lazily on its surface in the sunlight, sighing her contentment as the softest of warm breezes began to drift dreamily and enticingly across her body, making the tips of her breasts harden into rosy peaks under its slow caress and her soft thighs tremble.

And, as her entire body shivered with this new and astonishing pleasure, she thought—I want this never to end.

Yet end it did, and she turned languidly to swim for the side of the pool, but instead of the tiled edge she'd expected found her fingers clutching a pillow.

Her eyes snapped open. My God, she thought as she sat up, pushing her hair back from her face. I've been dreaming. How extraordinary.

Stranger still was the discovery that she was alone in the bed. But worst of all was the shocked realisation that she was naked, the nightshirt she'd been wearing lying in a crumpled heap on the floor.

She snatched it up with a gasp, holding it against her in a protective gesture that even she could see was totally useless.

He took it off, she thought, hot with embarrassment. Took it off when I was too deeply asleep to know what he was doing. And then he…

She swallowed. Well—at least it hadn't been *that*. She'd have to have been in a coma to sleep through a repeat of what he'd done to her the previous afternoon.

But that was small consolation when more details of that sweet and frankly sensuous dream were crowding back into her mind, and she couldn't be sure what was dream and what reality. Because something had created that delicate whisper of sensation across her body, which reason told her could only have been his hands—or even more disturbingly his mouth.

At least he wasn't here, she thought feverishly, so she didn't have to face him—wondering—knowing she could never ask.

She heard a chink of china from the corridor, signalling Hara's approach with her coffee, and tugged the shirt back on. It was far too late for her to worry about appearances, but, for reasons she couldn't explain even to herself, she knew she'd rather give the impression that Vassos had spent the night in his own room.

But Hara's attitude was briskly incurious as she poured the coffee. And she had some news of her own to impart.

'Kyrios Vassos go to Athens,' she announced. 'Go very early.'

'Oh.' Joanna was aware of an odd *frisson* which she told herself was relief not disappointment.

'Back tonight,' Hara added, as if offering consolation. 'Today you rest. Make yourself beautiful for him.' She went to the wardrobe and took a turquoise bikini from the selection in a drawer, producing a filmy thigh-length jacket in turquoise and gold to go over it. She gave Joanna a beguiling smile. 'You stay by pool, *ne?*'

Joanna sipped her coffee and decided to distract herself from the notion of making herself attractive for Vassos by introducing another topic.

'Perhaps,' she returned. 'I haven't decided.' She paused. 'Hara—who lives at the house in the olive grove?'

The jacket slipped off its hanger to the floor and the older woman bent to retrieve it. She straightened, looking flushed. 'Is not important, Kyria Joanna. Not a problem for you. Best to keep away.'

So I've been told, Joanna thought.

Aloud, she said, 'But it must be lonely there—especially for a small child. I might stroll over there later—play a game with her, or take her for a walk. Maybe bring her back to play in the pool.'

'*Ochi!*' Hara's vehemence was startling. 'No, *thespinis*. Not possible. The child belongs in other house, not here. Better you go to beach for walking.'

'Then perhaps I'll talk to—to Kyrios Vassos about it,' Joanna said, stumbling slightly over the unfamiliar name.

Hara's face assumed its former stony expression. 'No, *thespinis*. You must not speak of this. It is not permitted. There are things you do not understand.'

She placed the clothes she was holding on the dressing stool and hurried to the door.

Joanna watched it close after her, her initial bewilderment giving way to anger.

Not permitted? she echoed silently. No prizes for guessing who'd issued that edict. Hadn't the Greeks invented the word tyrant—a description clearly tailor-made for the owner of Pellas?

She could see now why Stavros had been so anxious to steer her away from the olive groves without actually forbidding her to go there.

Nothing to see indeed, she thought indignantly. Only human beings.

From what Hara had said, it seemed obvious that the girl and her baby had been put into virtual exile.

Another form of Gordanis revenge? she wondered bitterly. But what on earth could they have done to deserve it?

Things you do not understand…

She clattered her cup back on to its saucer.

'No, Hara,' she whispered under her breath. 'You're the one who doesn't understand. That little girl is scarcely more than a baby, so, whatever's happened, she's the innocent party in all this—and she's unhappy. Also lonely. I saw it in her eyes. And I knew she didn't want me to go.'

Although the mother wasn't neglectful in material ways. The

tot was clearly well-nourished, and her clothes were expensive if unsuitable.

But how much time did she actually spend with her, teaching her all the skills a growing child needed. Or simply talking—laughing with her? Making her feel loved and secure?

That's what really matters, Joanna told herself passionately. And while I'm around I'll make sure that's what she gets. And it will help me, too. Give me some kind of purpose in this life that's been forced on me.

She showered, dressed in a pair of white shorts and a jade-green tee shirt and went down to have breakfast. It seemed a more protracted meal than usual with Andonis hovering to ask if she would like a fresh pot of coffee—more hot rolls—grapes instead of nectarines.

Afterwards, he asked her if she'd enjoyed the honey that had come with the bowl of thick, creamy yoghurt, and, when she said in perfect truth that it was delicious, began telling her in detail how it had come from the bees his older sister Josefina kept on Thaliki.

After which Hara arrived, apparently to supervise the maids who were sweeping the other end of the terrace, and Joanna realised, lips tightening, that she was being watched.

Accordingly, she crammed on her hat, picked up her bag and set off ostentatiously in the direction of the cove. Once out of sight of the villa, she sat down on a convenient boulder, allowing some fifteen minutes to elapse before doubling back.

I feel like a character out of a thriller, she reflected, wrinkling her nose as she skirted the gardens and reached the olive trees without the alarm being raised.

She found her way to the house without difficulty, but there was no Eleni to be seen, playing in the garden or standing at the gate. In fact the whole place looked oddly deserted. She stood at the fence for a moment or two, listening to the silence, then tried the gate, only to find it locked. So that, she thought, would seem to be that.

Yet where could they possibly have gone—and so quickly? Had she been deliberately delayed over breakfast so that they could be moved on?

Ah, well, she thought with a soundless sigh. So much for my good intentions. She turned to go and paused as something seemed to flicker in the corner of her eye.

Was it her imagination or had a shutter moved at an upstairs window? She waited for a moment, gazing upwards, but all was still again, and with a small, defeated shrug Joanna went back the way she had come.

She spent the day quietly, reading in the shade of the terrace, trying not to think about Vassos' return, and what it would mean.

He did not return in time for dinner, and as she ate her solitary meal Joanna began to hope that he would remain in Athens overnight.

When she went to her bedroom, one of the new nightgowns was waiting for her on the bed. It was the most beautiful thing she'd ever seen, she thought numbly, gazing in the mirror at the simple column of cream satin, slashed to the thigh and falling from a wide band of lace which veiled her breasts without totally concealing them.

Even she could appreciate that, although Vassos had clearly bought it for his own delectation rather than hers.

Only he was not here to see it, she reminded herself thankfully, as she climbed into bed.

She was woken by a hand on her shoulder, and Hara's voice saying her name.

She sat up. 'What's wrong?'

'All is well, *thespinis*. Kyrios Vassos has returned and is asking for you.'

She almost said, But it's the middle of the night, remembering just in time that was probably exactly the point.

'Not good to make him wait,' Hara warned as Joanna slid reluctantly out of bed. She was holding a large shawl, fine and light as gossamer, which she wrapped briskly round the girl's shoulders before ushering her out of the room and down the corridor.

She paused before a pair of double doors, knocked, then turned the elaborate iron handle, indicating that Joanna should enter.

He was standing by the open window, looking out into the darkness, glass in hand. He was not wearing the crimson dressing gown, she saw with relief, but a simple white towelling robe. His hair was damp, and there was a faint hint of soap and some expensive cologne in the air.

He turned slowly and looked at her. *'Kalispera.'*

She held the shawl closer. 'Isn't it a little late for good evening?'

'I was delayed in Athens.' He drank some ouzo. 'Hara said you were sleeping. Were your dreams very sweet, *matia mou?'*

'I—I don't remember.' But an unwanted memory of what had invaded her rest the previous night brought swift colour to her face.

'Then I shall feel less guilty about waking you.'

'I doubt you even know what guilt is.'

He shrugged a shoulder. 'Perhaps I discovered it today when I listened to Petros trying to make excuses for all the lies he told about you, Joanna *mou.'* He added grimly, 'And about other matters.'

She looked down at the floor. 'I feel almost sorry for him.'

'After what he has done?'

'Yes,' she said in a stifled voice. 'Because it doesn't even compare with the misery you seem determined to inflict on me.'

'You were brought here to make amends, Joanna *mou,'* he said, after a slight pause. 'Perhaps I now wish to do the same.'

'Then let me go.' She stared at him in open appeal. 'I swear

I'll say nothing about what's happened. And if—anyone asks, I'll pretend you only ever meant to frighten me.'

'But I think I have indeed frightened you, *pedhi mou*. And hurt you also. I cannot let you go thinking that is how it must be between a man and his woman.'

'I am not your woman!'

'Not yet,' he corrected softly. 'But that is about to change.' He looked her over again, his mouth curving in sensuous appreciation, then drank the rest of his ouzo and put the tumbler down before he walked to her, parting the folds of the shawl and pushing it from her shoulders.

She heard him catch his breath sharply, then she was lifted into his arms and carried across to the vast bed which dominated the room, and which she had been trying so very hard to ignore.

He settled her against the mounded pillows and lay beside her. He pushed her hair back from her face, his thumb gently stroking her cheek, then slid one narrow satin strap from her shoulder, kissing the faint mark it had left on her skin.

The band of lace had slipped, too, baring one rounded breast, and he sighed against its scented flesh as he bent to take her nipple between his lips and caress it softly to unwilling but involuntary excitement.

This time it would be different, she thought. He expected to get pleasure from her and—unbelievably—to bestow it, too.

But she could not allow that to happen. She had to somehow keep her resolve to give nothing—and ask for nothing.

He raised his head, said her name softly, then kissed her, his mouth moving on hers with delicate, deliberate restraint. Reviving memories of the delicate dream-like caresses of the previous night.

It was she thought almost like a warning—signalling his determination to lead her slowly to a submission that she would be ultimately unable to resist.

Her task was to convince him all over again that he was wrong. That he could not arouse her to yield to him.

Having first convinced herself…

His fingers found the long slit in her gown and slipped inside, skimming over the smooth skin of her thigh before moving persuasively, subtly, up to her hip where they lingered.

His kiss deepened, coaxing her lips to part for him, reminding her that she could not afford the slightest intimacy. But how could she go on resisting when his hand was beginning to trace the slender planes and angles of her pelvis? Eliciting a quiver of response deep inside her that shocked her by its intensity. And scared her, too, because it threatened to weaken her resolve.

And then, quite suddenly, the kiss was ended, the hand removed.

'You are still fighting me?' Lying on his side, he watched her, his expression quizzical. Against the white robe, his skin looked darker than ever. Barbaric. 'Why?'

From somewhere she found the defence she so desperately needed. Forced the words from her throat. 'Because I hate you.'

'But I do not ask for love, *matia mou*,' he said softly. 'Just to teach you to need my body as much as I want yours.'

'That will never happen,' she said huskily, after a pause.

'No?' His smile was slow. 'You seem very sure.' He hooked a finger under the other strap of her nightgown, pulling it down and baring her breasts completely.

'And yet you do not seem completely immune,' he added, teasing each nipple in turn with a fingertip, watching them lift and harden at his touch, and sending a tremor of that same sharp sensation lancing through her entire body. 'Let me show you a little delight, my lovely one,' he whispered.

He pushed up the satin skirt, his hand stroking her slim thighs, then parting them without haste to discover the molten sweetness they sheltered.

Joanna stifled a gasp as she felt the sensual glide of his fin-

gers exploring her secret woman's flesh, her first experience
of such a seductive caress—and its devastating effect.

His fingertip found one moist silken place and teased the
tiny bud it hid, making it swell and bloom under his touch to
aching tumescence and her inner muscles contract in a scalding spasm of longing she'd never known could exist.

She was lost suddenly, breathless and drowning, then fighting her way back to the surface of her control with the last
drop of will-power she possessed.

She heard him whisper, 'I want you so much, *agapi mou*.
Don't make me take, when I wish so badly to give.'

His lips were gentle at the side of her neck, his hands sliding down to fondle her breasts with equal tenderness, touching them as if they were flowers.

She was aware of the throbbing heat of his erection, and
her pulses were going crazy, desire clenching inside her like
a fist.

How it must be...

He released her, turning away, and for a moment she thought
he was leaving the bed, but one glance over her shoulder revealed that he was only removing his robe, then reaching for
a drawer in the night table and making use of the contents of
a small packet he'd extracted from it.

As he had told her, he still intended to make her completely
his. And for one brief, desolate instant she remembered the
beguiling sensuous web he'd begun to weave for her, before
Vassos moved over her—into her—in urgent and breathtaking possession.

Making her realise that when his passion was spent, desolation was all that was left for her. And, what was worse, reminding her that she'd brought it entirely on herself.

CHAPTER TEN

IT SEEMED almost as if her body had been ready—even waiting—to be united with his. As if it was only the driving rhythm of his possession that could appease the throbbing ache now building slowly and insidiously far within her.

Tempting her to put her arms round him and offer her parted lips to the kisses she'd once denied him. To arch her body towards him, taking him ever more deeply into her in the ultimate surrender.

Above all to pursue and capture those incomprehensible but exquisite sensations that seemed to be hovering, tantalising her, just beyond her reach, and so discover for the first time the reality of passion's physical conclusion.

And then, just as Joanna realised, stunned, that this might be an actual possibility, it was suddenly over. She heard him cry out hoarsely and felt his body shudder into hers. For a moment he lay still, his face buried in her breasts, his slackened weight pressing her into the mattress, and Joanna conquered an impulse to lift a hand and stroke his sweat-dampened black hair.

How can I even think of something like that? she asked herself incredulously. When I hate him? And when I've told him so?

Yet was that really what she felt? Or did she only hate the senses that had so nearly betrayed her?

Before I met him I never knew, she thought. Never imagined—*how it must be...*

After a while Vassos moved, lifting himself silently away
from her. He got up from the bed, picked up his discarded
robe and walked across to a door she guessed must lead to his
bathroom.

As soon as she was alone, Joanna hastily adjusted her nightgown, pulling up the straps of the bodice and tugging the skirt
over her legs so that she was reasonably covered again. Then,
heart racing, she waited.

He was not gone for long. When he emerged, she saw thankfully that his robe was now wrapped round him. He came back
to the bed, not hurrying, and lay down beside her on his back,
his arms folded behind his head as he stared up at the ceiling.

He turned his head slowly and looked at her. 'I hope this
time you experienced less discomfort, and that you did not
find my demands too excessive?'

She touched the tip of her tongue to her dry lips. 'No, I—I
didn't.'

'Then that is a beginning at least,' he said. 'Even if not the
one I hoped for.'

She took a deep breath, trying desperately to pull herself
together. To regain control of her thoughts as well as her emotions. 'May I go now, please? Or do you—want...?'

'No,' he said harshly. 'You may leave.'

She slid off the bed, retrieving the shawl on her way to the
door, enfolding herself in its softness, even keeping it round
her as she climbed back into bed in her own room. It was far
too warm a night for it to be necessary but she found it oddly
comforting just the same.

But why should she need comfort? After all, she knew now
the worst to expect and it was—endurable, wasn't it? Or even
dangerously more than endurable, she thought, remembering
the seductive caress of his hands and lips as they'd gentled
her body, coaxing her towards the threshold of delight. And

if she had refused to cross it with him, she had only herself to blame. Or thank.

At any rate, it would not last for much longer. She was sure of that.

He'd made it clear that he had not found tonight particularly rewarding, she thought. So he would soon be looking for a more amenable girl to be—what had he called it?—a pillow friend.

She turned over restlessly, looking for a cooler place on her own pillow, which didn't seem friendly at all, remembering, as she did so, the previous night and how he'd held her, lulling her to sleep in spite of herself.

The way, too, that he'd caressed and fondled her gently while she slept. The touch of his hands and mouth on her skin tonight had totally convinced her of that, she thought, her body warming. Denial might be convenient but it was also pointless.

She was suddenly stifling in the shawl—and in the nightdress, too, she decided, stripping herself of them both. Even the sheet across her body was more than she could stand.

She was not just hot, either—she was on fire, every pulse beating a tattoo that echoed the throbbing hunger filling her innermost being, and that even her comparative innocence could recognise was unsatisfied longing. A renewed awakening of her flesh that had been ignited the first time he had lain with her.

I can't let myself want him, she told herself with a kind of desperation as her body twisted on the mattress. Not after the way he's treated me—after every terrible, vile thing that he's done. I must be going crazy even to contemplate it.

She sat bolt upright, trying to control the flurry of her breathing, to quell the tumult of her senses.

Sleep, she thought. Oh, God, I really need to get some sleep. Then, tomorrow, I can forget this madness and begin again.

But she soon found that was not going to be as easy as she'd hoped. Half an hour later she was still wide awake, staring into the darkness, the sheet beneath her damp with perspiration.

She put her hands flat on her breasts, touching them softly, tentatively. Feeling her nipples diamond-hard against her palms.

Is this how it's going to be—this agony of need each time? This longing for him to make me in some way—complete?

The questions beat at her brain, or at the brain of the stranger she had suddenly become. This creature of sensations and yearnings she did not even recognise.

Yet the alternative was to go to him—offer herself—and that was unthinkable. Wasn't it? Because what could she possibly say to him? What excuse could she give?

She gave a little shaken sigh. Maybe words would be unnecessary, and her presence, returning to lie beside him in the night, would be enough.

Moving like an automaton, she climbed off the bed, reaching down for the shawl, letting its soft folds settle round her nakedness.

She went to the door, but as she began to open it she heard not far away the quiet sound of another door closing and froze.

She peeped cautiously through the narrow opening and saw Vassos, clad in jeans and polo shirt, coming down the passage towards her. He strode past without even a glance in the direction of her room, and Joanna stood in the darkness, waiting until the sound of his rapid footsteps faded.

She went back to the bed and lay down, trembling, telling herself she should be thankful that she'd been spared the humiliation of arriving in his room to find it empty or—even worse—of bumping into him on his way out.

At the same time she found herself wondering where he could possibly be going at this time of night. And why...

But that, she thought, is not my concern. It simply means I've been saved at the last minute from making another terrible mistake. Persephone must have been watching out for me.

She pulled up the covering sheet and turned over, but it was more than two hours before she finally fell asleep, exhausted from the solitary vigil of lying in the darkness, listening for the sound of his return.

While some instinct she'd not known she possessed warned her that she waited in vain.

Joanna walked along the edge of the sea, small warm waves lapping round her feet. To a casual observer, if there'd been one about, she probably looked like a carefree girl in shorts and a sun top, happily enjoying a paddle in the sunshine.

Only she could know she was a seething mass of nerves.

It was a week since Vassos had walked past her and out into the night. Seven days and seven nights during which she'd been taught unequivocally just what it was to be the object of a man's passionate desire. And the exquisite agony of forcing herself to seem indifferent to his lovemaking.

He sent for her each night—that went without saying. But he also came to her room in the drowsy afternoon siesta hours. Their encounters were prolonged and almost magically sensuous, with Vassos, at times, almost fiercely intent on wringing some kind of erotic response from her trembling, fevered flesh, and at others enticing her with a tender yearning that almost stopped her heart, as if his whole body had been created as an instrument for her pleasure.

And Joanna lay beneath him, refusing to show any sign of emotion, even in the extremity of surrender when her desperate senses screamed for satisfaction.

He wanted to win, she reminded herself when she was once again alone. He'd won her at cards, and now he wished to complete his victory. His touch, his kisses, had one purpose—to prove that she was indeed a woman like any other in his experience. And if she thought he meant more, then she was fooling herself.

In one matter he was utterly scrupulous, however. He always used a sheath which, she supposed ruefully, was a kind of caring, if not the kind she had secretly begun to crave from him.

She was not proud of such blatant weakness, but she could not deny it, either. Whenever he was around she found she was watching him almost obsessively from behind the screen of her sunglasses, drinking in every inch of the lean body she'd once shrunk from.

But it was just sex—that was all, she assured herself almost feverishly. Nothing more. So there were no deeper feelings involved. How could there be when he would always be the man who'd kidnapped her in order to take her for revenge?

Yet he had somehow, against all the odds, made her want him in return so much that her mind seemed to ache as well as her body.

Sometimes, in the night, when she was back in her own room, she heard again the approach of his footsteps in the passage and sat up, lips parted breathlessly, staring at the door. Willing it to open. And, by some miracle, for everything to change.

But it never did. Instead Vassos simply walked on, leaving her still wondering. And sometimes crying inside.

Although she could admit now, in the brilliant sunshine, there were other matters apart from the strictly personal also preying on her mind.

For one thing, it had occurred to her that since her arrival no one, least of all Vassos himself, had mentioned his wife in any way.

And her visits to his bedroom had revealed at a glance that he wasn't treasuring as much as one solitary souvenir of the woman who'd once shared it with him.

It was almost, she'd decided, puzzled, as if the late Mrs Gordanis had never existed.

Perhaps, she thought, aware of a swift pang, he had loved her so much that he could not bear to be reminded, even marginally, of the happiness they'd enjoyed together.

In addition, there was also the matter of the mysterious

house in the olive grove, and its occupants, although Vassos' continuing presence had offered her no opportunity to return there and see if Eleni and her mother had returned—if, of course, they had ever been away.

But he'd left that morning to fly to Athens on business, so she would be alone for ten days or more, as he'd sardonically informed her. And she was going to need something to distract her in his absence—if only to protect her against missing him too much.

She folded her arms round her body, shivering a little in spite of the heat. It was still a shock that she could even admit to such feelings—or confess inwardly that she'd hoped against hope that he would invite her to accompany him on his trip.

As it was, she'd made sure she was awake especially early that morning, going out on to her balcony to listen for the sound of the high-speed launch that would take him across to Thaliki.

And she'd remained standing there long after the engine noise was no longer audible, staring at the azure glimmer of the sea in the distance over the top of the pines. Stared until her eyes blurred, and pressed a finger against her trembling mouth in case she called 'Don't leave me. Don't go,' into the empty air.

Just as a few hours before, when he lay against her in the aftermath of his climax, she had almost begged him, Don't send me away tonight. Let me stay with you. Make love to me again. Share with me what you feel. Teach me to be your woman at last.

But she had bitten back the words, because she still couldn't acknowledge, even to herself, that withholding her body had been useless. That from the very beginning, when he'd been no more than a pirate smiling at her from the deck of a yacht, it had been her heart that was really in danger.

And each time she lay in his arms, listening to the soft Greek words he whispered to her as his hands roamed her flesh with sensual expertise, she became more deeply lost in a longing that was so much more than physical.

Terrified that one night she might even whisper the words that must forever be taboo between them. *I love you...*

'I didn't want this,' she whispered in wretchedness. '*I don't want this.* Because I've no idea how to deal with it. Or with him. Or what I shall do when he decides to end it.'

But at least she no longer feared that he would pass her on to another man, as he'd originally threatened to do. That, she supposed, was something she had to be thankful for.

And another positive move would be to stop tormenting herself like this over a situation that she could not change and instead try to assuage her own loneliness and heartache with another attempt to help a solitary child who needed a friend.

She walked out of the water, wincing a little as her feet encountered the hot sand, balancing quickly on one leg and then the other in order to resume the espadrilles she was carrying.

As she did so, she realised she was not alone. That one of the security guards was stationed in the shade of the trees, watching her. As she walked up the beach towards the track he straightened, throwing away the cigarette he'd been smoking.

Now, where had he sprung from? she asked herself, annoyed.

His name was Yanni, and he was the only one of Vassos' watchdogs that she'd come to dislike. The others faded away politely at her approach, but Yanni always grinned insolently when he saw her, and she seemed to encounter him in all kinds of unlikely places.

Joanna was conscious of his gaze following her now as she started up the track. But he never spoke to her, so there was no real complaint she could make about him. She just knew she was glad when the bend in the path took her out of his line of vision.

She wandered casually through the gardens, in case her

progress was being marked from the house, but all seemed quiet, and she was soon in the welcome concealment of the olive trees.

As their peace closed round her again, it occurred to her that there were times when her life with Vassos assumed a kind of normality. When they actually talked together. Had real conversations. Although these generally occurred over the meals they shared on the terrace.

She recalled he'd spoken one evening of all the miles his work caused him to travel, and how he always waited with impatience to return home.

'But why here?' she'd asked, greatly daring.

'Look around you,' he said. 'It is very beautiful, although you, of course, cannot be expected to find it so.'

Yet I could, she thought, if things were different. Then caught herself guiltily, knowing she was straying into forbidden territory.

She'd shrugged. 'It's certainly very secluded. Why is that?'

'It was my grandfather's decision.' Vassos played with the stem of his wine glass. 'He was first a businessman, but also a scholar. His chief study was the ancient mythology of our country, and for that he required privacy. So when he found Pellas and bought it, he made sure it was his alone.'

She almost said, But what about the house in the olive grove? but stopped herself just in time.

'When the Germans came during the war, they considered it too small to be of strategic importance,' he went on. 'So my mother was able to take refuge here when my father joined the partisans. And I was born here.'

'And you've always lived here?' Once more she thought about his wife.

'Here,' he said. 'Or on the *Persephone*.' His mouth twisted. 'There have been times in my life when it was safer to keep moving.'

'I wish,' she said, 'that my father had felt the same way.'

'Do you, *pedhi mou?*' He sent her a meditative look across the candles. 'Well, perhaps you cannot be blamed.' He paused. 'You are shivering a little. Let us go into the *saloni* and listen to some music.'

Usually it was classical music, drawn from a range of composers from Mozart to Stravinsky. Sometimes he chose the insistent beat of Greek bouzouki. But that night he'd slotted a very different tape into the deck, and Joanna recognised with astonishment some of the tracks she'd danced to at the last school disco, in an emerald mini-skirt and the platform shoes that Jackie had loaned her because Gail had refused point-blank to let her have a pair, maintaining she'd sprain her ankle or worse.

She gave a swift sigh and Vassos looked at her, brows lifting. 'You don't like this tune?'

'No, I love it.' She shook her head. 'It just brought back—a memory, that's all.'

The tape moved into the soft insidious rhythm of Donna Summers' 'Love to Love You, Baby', and Vassos rose and came across to her. 'And this also?' he queried.

'Well—no.'

He switched off the central light, leaving the room lit by a single lamp, before taking her hand and pulling her to her feet. 'Then let us create a new one.'

For a moment she hesitated, self-conscious, because it was a long time since she'd danced and her male partners had been few anyway.

Then the music took her and she began to move in shy enticement, matching the lithe grace of the man dancing a couple of feet away from her. The man who reached for her and sent her spinning away from him, then brought her back, close to him, his hands clasping her hips, her fingers splayed across the warmth of his shoulders through the fine linen of his shirt. The man she longed to kiss her as the music ended. To kiss her and carry her to his bed as the song seemed to promise.

But he had not done so, Joanna thought as she looked up at

the rustling silvery leaves of the olive trees and felt her throat tighten. And, for the first time, that night she had spent entirely alone.

When she arrived at the house, she saw Eleni in the garden, listlessly pushing a little pram with a doll in it up and down the path. This time she was wearing a yellow lace dress which struck Joanna as even less suitable or becoming than the last one.

She walked to the gate, smiling. '*Kalimera,* Eleni.'

The child paused warily, and her thumb stole to her mouth.

Joanna went down on her haunches, her smile widening in warm encouragement. 'Do you remember me? From the other day?' She pointed at herself. 'Joanna.'

There was a silence, then Eleni made a first hesitant attempt at the name.

'Well done.' Joanna laughed and clapped her hands. She was rewarded with a smile from the little girl, fugitive at first, then more confident, lighting up the small face in a way that seemed curiously familiar. And which tugged all too potently at her heartstrings.

'You again.' The voice came sharply from behind her, and Joanna rose and turned to confront the child's mother, who'd apparently emerged from another part of the grove and was standing, hands on hips, her sloe eyes snapping.

She was wearing a blue dress today, its bodice buttoned awry over her full breasts and the skirt creased. Her hair looked dishevelled and she was holding a lighted cigarette.

Looking a mess was one thing, Joanna thought, her mouth tightening. Going off on some errand, leaving Eleni to play alone, was quite another.

She took a deep breath, keeping her smile resolutely in place. '*Kalimera, kyria,*' she returned politely.

'Why you here, Gordanis' woman?' The demand was sulky. 'He send you? Why he not come?'

Joanna bit her lip. 'Kyrios Gordanis is away—on business in Athens.'

'Athens, *po, po, po*. Maybe he has woman there. Real woman,' she added scornfully. 'No pale—no skinny like you.'

Joanna felt her colour rise. 'Maybe,' she agreed evenly. 'But I came to visit Eleni, not discuss Kyrios Gordanis' affairs.'

'Why you visit?' The woman came nearer, tossing away her cigarette end. 'You think you make friend of daughter her papa like you better, *ne?*' The full mouth curled. 'I don't think so.'

Joanna was very still. 'Her—papa?' she repeated slowly.

'You not know?' There was real malice now. 'You make baby with Gordanis, *anglitha,* be sure you give him son, or he build house for you, hide you and girl baby, too. Forget her.'

Joanna wanted to cry out, I don't believe you. You're lying.

Instead, she turned and looked at Eleni, and saw the solemn mouth curve once more into that slow, entrancing smile. And knew, with a sinking heart, why it had seemed so familiar.

Realised, too, why she had been warned to keep away. Because she'd been intended to remain in total ignorance about Vassos' discarded mistress and her forgotten illegitimate child. His unwanted daughter.

She said quietly, 'I understand. I—I'm sorry I intruded.'

The girl came nearer. Her voice became ingratiating. 'You tell Gordanis that Soula say come see his girl. Each day I dress her—make fine for her papa. Each day he stay away—see his friends—his women. Not her. Never her. She cry. He not hear. Not care.' She paused. 'You come, *thespinis.* Talk—play with Eleni—so you can say to him how good, how pretty. Maybe in bed he listen to you.'

Words of instant negation rose to Joanna's lips, but when she looked back at Eleni she knew they would never be uttered. That she could not simply walk away and not return—no matter now much hurt this unbearable truth might be causing her.

Because there was a small, vulnerable girl who was being hurt far more. Who needed the companionship and care that neither her father nor her mother seemed prepared to offer.

And for that reason she could not turn her back.

She said abruptly, 'I'll come back tomorrow, *kyria*. Teach her to play a game with her ball. But not those clothes, please. Shorts and a tee shirt.'

To the child, watching hopefully through the gate, she said more gently, searching for the Greek words, '*Avro, Eleni. Endaxi?*' Then turned swiftly and went before she could be tormented by another glimpse of that smile.

She walked fast, head bent, staring down at the ground with eyes that saw nothing.

Vassos, she thought, pain twisting inside her. How could you do this—you with your sense of family? Your own child—your little girl—how can you keep her here and ignore her even if you no longer want her mother?

Nothing you've done to me is anywhere near as cruel as this.

She thought of Eleni waiting each day. Hoping…

All dressed up and nowhere to go.

She shook herself, forcing back her tears.

Well, that child was not going to end up emotionally damaged if she had anything to do with it.

When Vassos returned she would confront him. Brave his undoubted anger and remind him of his paternal responsibilities. Tell him that, for one thing, his daughter was sometimes left completely alone in that deserted spot.

If her mother's not prepared to look after her properly, he should employ a nanny, she told herself.

For a moment she was haunted by an image of Vassos and his former mistress together, passionately entwined, and bit her lip hard as she wondered how they had met and become involved.

Soula might have grown blowsy since that time, but she was still good-looking in a blatantly sensual way, and Joanna could see why he would have been attracted.

Although that did not necessarily mean he'd intended their association to result in a child or welcomed the birth when it came.

But it does explain why he's so careful to use contraceptives when we're together, she told herself forlornly. It's not to protect me, but to ensure that he doesn't repeat his mistake.

'And does it also follow that you have no wish to bear me a child?'

His words—making it seem as if the decision was hers.

She found herself wondering why this total estrangement from Soula had come about. Had he become ashamed of the liaison, aware that he'd let his body rule his brain? Or had it ended with some tumultuous quarrel which had turned him implacably against his former lover?

Whatever the cause, it's hardly likely he'll ever discuss it with me, Joanna thought, sighing. Because Vassos didn't account for his actions. He just—decided, and that was it. I'm the living proof of that.

She stopped for a moment, leaning against the trunk of an olive tree, aware of the scrape of its gnarled bark through her thin clothing.

But she'll still know as much about him as I do, she thought wretchedly. Will be aware of every intimate detail. The birthmark like a tiny dark rose on his shoulderblade. The heat, the strength of him as he moves to his climax and the huskiness in his voice when he comes.

Each time I see her I'll have to remember that, and learn somehow to endure it. But I also have to think of Eleni shut behind that gate on her own. It's her well-being that has to matter now, not my jealousy of her mother or her resentment of me.

And if I can somehow persuade Vassos that his daughter needs him, and doesn't deserve to be hidden away like this, then perhaps my time here won't be such a complete disaster after all.

And if I keep telling myself that, I may even come to believe it.

CHAPTER ELEVEN

'KYRIOS VASSOS sent another radio message this morning, *thespinis*.' There was reproof in Stavros' voice. 'He wished to speak to you. Asked that you be fetched.' He paused. 'I had to tell him once again that you could not be found.'

'I went for a walk,' Joanna returned evenly, replacing her empty coffee cup on its saucer. 'He can hardly expect me to hang around the house all day in case he makes contact.'

The expression on Stavros' face indicated that was probably exactly what his employer required.

He said heavily, 'If you were at the pool or on the beach, *thespinis*, there would not be a problem.' He paused again. 'But, as we all know, you are not. And when Kyrios Vassos returns he will ask questions.'

'Which I shall answer, and then ask a few of my own,' Joanna said crisply.

Stavros looked anguished. 'You must not—cannot do such things. You concern yourself in matters you do not understand, and you risk much anger.'

'On the contrary, I know exactly what I'm doing, and why. Besides, your boss is not the only one with a temper,' she added recklessly.

And my being in love with him does not make him right all the time, she thought, watching Stavros trudge despondently away.

She poured herself more coffee and sat back, looking out across the moonlit garden.

She'd known from the start, of course, that her prolonged daily absences would be noted and conclusions drawn, and she'd already run the gauntlet of reproachful looks and muttered remarks from Hara and Andonis.

But this was the first time she'd been openly challenged about where she spent her time and its possible consequences.

Although it's not all unalloyed delight for me, either, she thought with a faint sigh.

She had not anticipated that Soula would make her welcome, but she hadn't foreseen quite the level of sneering contempt that would greet her every time she appeared at the house. And she knew that, if it hadn't been for Eleni's growing delight in her company, she might well have given up.

Soula was no great housekeeper, either, and to judge by the amount of cigarette butts in the saucer on the living room table each day, she smoked like two factory chimneys.

Her cooking was marginally better, however, and there was usually a pot of reasonably palatable stew on the stove, and a batch of fresh bread.

The real bonus, however, was her habit of absenting herself, sometimes for a couple of hours or more, as soon as Joanna and Eleni had settled into their routine. She never offered any explanation for her disappearances and Joanna didn't ask for one, either, especially as Eleni seemed far more relaxed while her mother was away.

The language barrier was less of a problem than she'd envisaged. Eleni, once she was less shy, proved to be a bright child, with an enquiring mind and a reasonable vocabulary. By using picture books or simply pointing to things Joanna was able to expand her own knowledge of Greek and teach the little girl the English equivalent. Eleni's physical co-ordination was improving rapidly, too, now that she was allowed to run about without any frilly frocks to dirty or damage.

There was a pile of colouring books and drawing pads and

a box of crayons all unused and gathering dust on a shelf in the living room, plus a tub of Play-Doh, and Joanna used those to keep Eleni entertained indoors in the heat of the day. She also made sure that the child had a short rest after her lunch, overcoming her initial resistance by singing her softly to sleep, usually with 'Ten Green Bottles'.

At other times they were outside, either with the ball, or playing hilarious games of hide and seek and tag among the olive trees. In a large shed at the rear of the house, home to an elderly and disused olive press, Joanna also discovered a small tricycle, still in its original wrappings, and under her guidance Eleni soon learned to master it.

Best of all, the little face peering through the gate each morning was no longer wistful but bright-eyed and eager.

At the same time, the imminence of Vassos' return from Athens was never far from Joanna's mind, together with the inevitable row that would follow once he discovered how she'd been using her time. If, of course, he didn't already know.

The possibility that he might be angry enough to send her away had occurred to her, too. Especially as she'd offered him no incentive to keep her around, she reminded herself wryly.

Sighing, she pushed her chair back and rose. She'd finished yet another book, this time James Clavell's *Shogun,* and needed something new to read in bed. Something sufficiently absorbing, she reflected, to see her through yet another restless, miserable night.

She walked into the *saloni* and stood for a moment, listening to the silence all around her.

The Villa Kore seemed so terribly empty without Vassos' vigorous presence. She had become so swiftly accustomed to the sound of his quick stride, his voice calling to someone. The occasional burst of impatience when an order had not been carried out to his satisfaction. All of it so much a part of him.

I miss him so much, she thought. Want him so dearly. And I always shall, no matter what he is or what he has done.

I never dreamed how I would ache for his lips. Hunger for the touch of his hands on my skin. Long for him to caress me as he did that first night when I lay in his arms.

Nor did I ever realise—how could I?—how precious those brief moments of actual possession would become—especially as they are all I may ever have of him. All he will permit.

Oh, God, she thought with a pang of sadness, it was so much easier to hate him. And made so much more sense.

Vassos Gordanis. Absolute ruler of his domain, and the man she had chosen to defy—not just in his bedroom but by openly ignoring his explicit instructions.

But I won't think about it now, she told herself. There'll be time enough for that when he returns.

Won't there?

She chose a book almost at random, and went out to the stairs. She paused at their foot, looking at the statue of Persephone.

Was that why you ate the pomegranate seeds? she asked silently. To give you an excuse to stay with your own Dark Lord—because you, too, had learned to love him? Because you knew your life would always be winter without him?

And she shivered as she went up to her room for yet another night alone.

It was late the following afternoon when Joanna eventually made her way back through the olive grove.

Almost as soon as she'd arrived at the house Soula had disappeared, staying away this time until Joanna had begun to glance uneasily at her watch.

'Where have you been?' she'd asked sharply when, at last, the Greek girl came sauntering back through the trees, smoking the inevitable cigarette. 'I thought you were never coming.'

Soula shrugged, unperturbed. She looked, Joanna thought, relaxed and almost cheerful for once. 'Is a problem? Then why you not go? Leave Eleni in garden.'

'Because I would never do that,' Joanna returned icily. 'And nor should you.'

'Is safe,' the other retorted. 'What harm to Gordanis' child on Gordanis' island?' She paused, giving Joanna a speculative glance. 'You come back tomorrow, *anglitha?*'

Joanna swallowed her anger at Soula's cavalier attitude to childcare. 'Yes,' she said shortly. 'I'll be here. And then I think we need to have a talk, *kyria*.'

Eleni's small fingers caught a fold on her skirt and held it while she whispered something.

'She asks you promise,' Soula translated.

Joanna ran a hand over the child's springing dark hair. 'Tomorrow,' she said softly. 'I promise.'

There was a reception committee consisting of Stavros, Hara and Andonis drawn up on the terrace at the villa, and as soon as Joanna saw them she knew.

She halted. 'Kyrios Vassos?' she asked, looking from one grave face to another, aware of the unsteady thud of her heart against her ribcage.

Stavros gave the sideways tilt of his head that signified assent.

'He is waiting for you, *thespinis*.'

He did not add, 'And has been doing so for some time,' because he didn't have to. It was implicit in the way they were all looking at her. In their obvious apprehension.

And Joanna didn't have to ask where to find him, either. She just walked into the villa and went straight to his study.

Not a job interview this time, she thought, smoothing her damp palms down her skirt as she reached his door, which was standing ajar. Probably dismissal without notice or a reference.

She pushed the door open, and went into the room.

Vassos was standing at the window, his tall figure like a statue carved from obsidian against the deep afternoon sun. He did not move as she entered, and, after a moment, she said his name softly and tentatively.

He turned then, his gaze sweeping her, his mouth a hard line. She could feel the anger in him reaching out across the room to her like a clenched fist.

Fear dried her mouth as it had on the night of the poker game, but it was important not to let him see that. Because in that way he would gain the upper hand, and make it impossible for her to say all the things that she knew must be said.

'So,' he said. 'You have returned.'

'You—asked for me?' She kept her tone level.

'I sent for you,' he corrected harshly. 'I am told that you have been meddling, *thespinis*. Interfering in matters that are not your business, and doing so against my expressed wish. But that ends now. You will not go to the house of the olive press again. Let that be clearly understood.'

Joanna lifted her chin. 'My understanding is rather different. I believe that a child who is lonely and possibly neglected should be everyone's business, Kyrios Gordanis.'

'Enough!' His tone was molten. 'It is not a subject for discussion. I have given you an order, Joanna. You would be wise to obey it.'

'In this case I think I prefer compassion to wisdom,' she flung back at him. 'You once had some very hard words to say, here in this room, about my father, and how he'd allowed me to be treated. The dangers I'd been subjected to. Well, let me tell you that your own ideas on fatherhood win no prizes either, Kyrios Vassos. In fact, you're far worse, for you've chosen to ignore your child's existence completely, presumably because you no longer want her mother.'

Vassos came round the desk towards her, his dark eyes blazing, but Joanna stood her ground defiantly.

'And if Denys was rarely around,' she went on, 'I had a mother who loved and took care of me all the time I was growing up. Soula can't even be bothered to play with your daughter or teach her basic things. What's more, she vanishes for whole chunks of the day, leaving Eleni alone in the middle of nowhere. You may not think that matters, but I do.'

She swallowed. 'As parents, the two of you are a total disaster, and it's that lovely little girl who's suffering. I'm not going to abandon her to suit some—tyrannical whim of yours.'

Vassos had halted and was staring at her as she reached the end of her breathless tirade, his eyes narrowing in disbelief.

'Soula?' he grated. 'You think that Soula is Eleni's mother? That she was my mistress? Are you insane?'

Joanna felt as if she'd been winded. 'Not Soula's child?' she managed. 'Then—whose?'

There was a silence, then Vassos said with cold reluctance, 'The child was born to my late wife, Ariadne Philipou, several months after our marriage. The identity of the man who fathered her is still unknown to me.'

'But Soula says it's you,' Joanna protested. 'And that's what she tells Eleni, too. Lets her think that you're her papa and one day you'll come to see her.'

'Then she lies cruelly—on both counts,' he returned implacably. 'She is making a fool of you, Joanna, for some purpose of her own. A situation that will be dealt with,' he added ominously.

He turned away, walking back to the window. 'My wife died of a brain haemorrhage shortly after the birth of her daughter,' he went on, his words staccato. 'And because I could not bring myself either to acknowledge her lover's bastard as mine or admit the shameful truth, I let it be thought that the baby, too, had not survived. That I had suffered a double loss. *Theos!*' His brief laugh jarred bitterly. 'What a joke. What an eternal nightmare of a joke.'

Stricken, Joanna tried to say his name, but her lips could not frame the word.

'I had the baby brought quietly to Pellas,' Vassos continued after a pause. 'And established her at the house belonging to the old olive press, with the woman who had been my wife's maid and probable accomplice in her affair. So Soula knows the truth, whatever story she may spin now.'

He swung back and looked at Joanna, his face a bronze, unyielding mask.

'Now do you wonder, *thespinis,* why I do not visit the child? I feed, clothe and provide for her, but that is all. She is too potent a reminder of my life's worst mistake and the woman who betrayed me.'

'But that can't be right.' Joanna's voice was barely a whisper. 'Vassos, Eleni must be your child. She—she's just like you. She even looks at me with your smile.'

There was a silence. She saw his mouth tighten, then he said quietly, 'Can you be so sure? The good God knows there have been few enough smiles between us, Joanna *mou.*'

She said haltingly, 'But I think enough for me to remember—and recognise.'

He raised his eyebrows, clicking his tongue in negation. 'Maybe the resemblance you see is of your own imagining, because you wish it to be so. I know it is not possible.'

'If you'd just go to the house,' she begged. 'See for yourself.'

'There is no point.' His tone hardened. 'My bride taunted me with the news of her pregnancy on our wedding night, just after the consummation of our marriage had revealed that she was by no means the innocent virgin her father had claimed.'

'She told you—that?' Chilled with bewilderment, Joanna wrapped her arms round her body. 'Oh, how could she?'

He shrugged. 'We were not marrying for love, Joanna *mou,*' he said cynically. 'It was not a romance. Our union had been arranged as part of a much wider business arrangement with the Philipou organisation. My father told me bluntly it was time my bachelor existence, however enjoyable, came to an end, and I accepted that. Therefore Ariadne and I were acquainted, but no more. However, you must believe that I intended to treat her gently and with the respect her purity deserved once she became my wife. She, on the other hand, made it clear that she wished to punish me because I was not the man she wanted.

'Her confession had the desired result. I left her bedroom and never returned, while the amount of time we spent in each other's company afterwards can be counted in hours and minutes rather than days. But neither of us knew that she had a serious health problem, although it seems she complained of headaches from time to time.' He spread his hands. 'Now you know it all. But it changes nothing,' he added warningly. 'You should not have involved yourself with the child Eleni, and you will not do so again.'

Joanna looked down at the floor. She said with difficulty, 'I know I spoke harshly to you just now. I realise you don't deserve it, and I—I'm sorry for the things I said. I—didn't understand.'

'No,' he said bitterly. 'In truth, Joanna, you understand very little.' He paused. 'However, I will instruct Stavros to deal with the matters you have brought to my attention. It may be that the child would be better in the care of a respectable family on Thaliki, although they will need to be well paid for their discretion.'

'But whatever her mother did, Eleni isn't to blame.' Joanna looked at him pleadingly. 'She's an innocent party in all this. And what she needs more than anything is some real family life.' She hesitated. 'What about her grandfather? Mr Philipou? Wouldn't he take her?'

'He died six weeks after the wedding, in bed with his mistress,' Vassos said curtly. 'My own father died two years ago, believing I was a childless widower, and that is how it remains. I have taken financial responsibility for Ariadne's child. I shall do no more. And nor will you, so there is nothing further to discuss.' He walked to his desk and sat down. 'I will see you at dinner.'

'But I promised Eleni I would go back tomorrow,' Joanna said desperately. 'So, please may I do so—even if it's only to say goodbye? I—I can't break my word. Not to a child.'

Vassos looked at her with hauteur, his dark brows drawing together. 'You had no right to give such a promise,' he said coldly. 'And my decision is made. Perhaps you will think of the consequences in future before you interfere in affairs that do not concern you.' And he drew a file towards him and opened it, signalling the end of the interview.

She said very quietly, 'Vassos—I beg you. Have a little mercy. I—I'm all she's got.'

'That is hardly an argument to use with me, *matia mou*.' He did not look at her. 'Saying you can be generous with a child who is a stranger to you when you have given me less than nothing. Perhaps you have not considered that mercy can work both ways.'

He added politely, 'And now, if you will excuse me, I have work to do.'

She said numbly, 'Yes—yes, of course.' And left him, the dismissive words 'less than nothing' still burning in her brain.

And they were still there, tormenting her, hours later as she lay in bed, watching the moonlight make patterns on her tiled floor through the slatted shutters and waiting for the summons to his room that she knew now was not going to come.

The evening, as a whole, had not gone well, starting with her realisation that the table on the terrace was set for three and Stavros would be joining them for dinner.

It was not the first time it had happened, of course, but she'd thought that, after this time apart, Vassos would wish to be alone with her.

Instead she had sat, toying with her food, while the two men spoke softly to each other in their own language, their faces serious and purposeful. When the meal ended, Stavros rose, bade her a punctilious goodnight, and went. And almost at once Vassos excused himself quietly, saying he had work to finish, and left, too.

Leaving her without the chance she'd hoped for to begin to put right all the things that had gone wrong between them earlier. The assumptions she'd made—the accusations she'd levelled—had given him every right to be angry with her. She accepted that.

Soula duped me, she thought, and as a result I simply fooled myself into seeing a resemblance that didn't exist. Maybe—as Vassos said—I wanted it to be so, and it became so.

That must be how it happened.

And yet—and yet...

She stopped there. It was no good wishing that things were different. That she could wave a magic wand and make everything right. She had to deal with her life here as it was.

But at the same time she knew that she needed to try to find a chink in the wall of bitterness he'd built around himself after the appalling events of his marriage.

To repair the damage, somehow, and in doing so perhaps find again the man who'd held and caressed her with such astonishing tenderness.

The man she'd deliberately rejected to protect herself from the truth of her own feelings. A truth she could not admit in words.

He'd spoken of mercy, she thought. But instead she would offer him warmth, desire and passion, letting him see in this long-delayed surrender how deeply she'd yearned for him.

She slid out of bed, shrugging off her nightgown and letting it fall to the floor. She wrapped herself in the shawl, and walked in barefoot silence the length of the passage to Vassos' room.

She'd thought he would be asleep, but he was sitting propped up by pillows, reading more documents by the light of his bedside lamp.

As she hesitated just inside the door, he looked at her, brows lifting.

He said quietly, 'I did not invite you to join me.'

'Nevertheless I'm here.' She paused, aware this was not what she'd expected, adding uncertainly, 'Do you want me to leave?'

The dark eyes surveyed her, lingering on the lines of her

slender body which the cobweb veiling of the shawl did little to conceal.

'No,' he said, a faint smile playing about his mouth as he put his papers on the night table. 'Perhaps, after all, I do not.'

In obedience to his brief, imperative gesture, Joanna dropped the shawl and walked naked to the bed. She was blushing as she did so, but her gaze did not waver from his.

She lifted the cover of the single sheet and slid on to the mattress beside him.

He turned on to his side, propping himself on an elbow. His voice was even. 'What are you doing here, Joanna?'

She played with the embroidered hem of the sheet. 'Maybe I don't like sleeping by myself.'

'Yet when I have been here you have done so every night except one.' He sounded almost matter-of-fact.

Her flush deepened. 'Yes, I know that. But we've been apart for over a week. I thought you might have—missed me.'

'You assume then that I also spent my nights alone during my time in Athens?' He sounded amused.

For a moment Joanna felt winded, as if she'd been abruptly rammed in the stomach by a fist.

She swallowed, controlling the sudden anguished flurry of her breathing. Fighting the flare of pain his casual remark had ignited.

She said in a low voice, 'You indicated this afternoon that I should learn to mind my own business. Therefore, I have no right to know what you do when you're—away from me. Or even to ask.'

And, hardest of all, no right to care...

'My congratulations,' he gibed. 'It seems you have mastered one lesson at least. Now, why are you really here?'

She was silent for a long moment, then she said, her voice quivering a little, 'Perhaps to acquire a—different kind of knowledge.'

She touched his bare shoulder with fingers that trembled, letting them trace an uneven trail down his chest.

Vassos drew a sharp breath, then took the edge of the concealing sheet and tossed it away, down to the foot of the bed, leaving them naked together in the lamplight.

She was assailed by the thought of the sophisticated and experienced women who had been his lovers in the past. Maybe, she thought unhappily, in the very recent past, as he'd hinted. And what did she have to offer? she asked herself as nervousness mingled with a sense of her own gaucherie almost overwhelmed her.

When she spoke, her voice shook. 'I thought that you...'

'Oh, no, *pedhi mou*. If, at last, you truly wish to know how the joining of a man and a woman can touch the edge of Paradise, then you must discover this for yourself. Seduce me as at first I tried to seduce you.'

She said wretchedly, 'But I don't know how. I—I don't know anything...'

'It is not so difficult.' His voice gentled. 'Unlike a woman, Joanna *mou,* I cannot hide the fact that I want you. So you can only win. And, as a beginning, you could kiss me.'

He reached for her, drawing her close and winding his fingers in her hair as he brought her mouth slowly to his.

Her lips were shy as they touched him, but she had the remembered gentleness of his own first kisses—the offered tenderness to guide her as her mouth moved softly, persuasively on his, caressing the firm contours of his lips until finally she coaxed them to part for her, her body melting at the honeyed sweetness of his tongue gliding against hers.

As their kiss deepened, became more urgent, Joanna slid her arms round his neck, arching her body against him so that the already sensitive peaks of her breasts grazed his chest in aching tumescence, and, in turn, she felt the steel hardness of his erection surge against her in unspoken demand.

She was drowning in her longing for him, scalding in the liquid heat of her own desire. Desperate to take him inside her and surrender to the promised consummation of her need.

But some instinct told her not yet. Wait a little. And, in

obedience to its compulsion, she began to press tiny, fleeting kisses to the strong column of his throat. Swift, teasing contacts that would arouse but not satisfy, she thought from some warm, dazed corner of her mind, wondering how she could possibly know this.

At the same time she allowed her hands to slide across the width of his shoulders, then move with lingering emphasis down the lean strong body, following the dark shadowing of hair from his chest to his stomach and beyond. And where her hands touched, her mouth followed.

Vassos lay back, his eyes closed, his body taut under the silken passage of her fingers and lips. He did not speak, but the sharp indrawn breath he could not control told her better than words of the effect her untutored caresses were having.

And when she reached the proud male shaft, encircling its heated, jutting power in the clasp of her hand and stroking it gently, she heard him give a hoarse groan of pleasure.

He turned to her, his mouth seeking hers, invading it in passionate demand, while his hands cupped her breasts, fondling their delicate curves, stirring her to a delight that was almost pain as his fingers teased her engorged nipples.

Her arms went round him, her hands exploring the long, graceful back and flat, muscular buttocks, and he smiled into her eyes as his hand slid down between her parted thighs to discover the burning moisture of her surrender and to explore it with heart-stopping eroticism.

Joanna gasped against his lips as his questing fingertip penetrated the satin folds of her secret woman's flesh to find her tiny hidden bud and caress it to a pinnacle of aching, soaring arousal.

Every nerve-ending in her skin seemed to be coming searingly alive under the rhythmic certainty of his touch—every sense, every atom of feeling in the core of her being gloriously coalescing into some unimagined and unimaginable culmination.

She felt herself poised on an unknown brink, and from some

distant space she heard her own husky whisper—'Please—oh, please...'

Heard his own hoarse response, *'Agapi mou.'*

And in the next instant found herself overtaken and overwhelmed by the piercing, shuddering wonder of her first climax.

As the pulsations reached their peak, Vassos' hands closed on her slender waist, lifting her over him, then lowering her on to him with infinite care until his hard, virile strength was totally sheathed inside her, forcing a small sob of delight from her quivering lips.

And Joanna, obeying the same instinct that had guided her before, began to move on him, with him, her inner muscles still clenching powerfully and sweetly around him, and her sensitised skin responding rapturously to the warm drift of his hands on her breasts, her belly, her hips and down to the shadowed cleft of her thighs.

Aware of the intensity of his half-closed eyes as they watched the sway of her slim body above her, and the harsh sigh of his breathing.

She heard it quicken almost hectically, then Vassos flung back his head, his skin dewed with sweat, the veins standing out on his neck, and a sound that might have been her name was torn from his throat as she felt him spasm fiercely inside her.

She slumped forward, burying her face in his damp shoulder as she yielded to the delicious languor enveloping her.

They lay wrapped together for a while, until the wild spinning of the world returned to normality and their breathing steadied, then Vassos moved slowly, detaching himself from her.

There was a long silence, then he said quietly and coolly, 'So, Joanna *mou,* having pleasured me so exquisitely, have you nothing to ask from me in return? Some favour, perhaps?'

Only—how soon can we do this again? Joanna reflected,

blushing a little. Then paused, wondering, because surely he must know the pleasure had been completely mutual.

She said aloud, 'I—I don't understand what you mean.'

'No? Yet it is surely quite simple. You want my permission to visit the child Eleni, as you requested this afternoon. And you are determined to have your way. After all, what else could have prompted the ardour of such a performance?'

He added silkily, 'I do not complain, you understand. But I must also be realistic. You wished to buy my acquiescence by offering me the only coin you thought I would accept. But you should be more subtle in your trading, *pedhi mou*. Because, in spite of this delightful and astonishing interlude, my answer to your request still remains—no. And as I shall not change my mind, no matter what further enticements you offer, you may prefer now to return to your own room. But please believe I shall always be—grateful.'

CHAPTER TWELVE

JOANNA stared at him, stunned. For a moment her mind ran riot as she told herself he could not be serious—could not possibly mean those unkind, cynical remarks that he'd almost negligently tossed at her.

Not after what had just happened between them—surely? All that passion and glory reduced to the level of a—trade-off? It couldn't be true.

But there was none of the former tenderness in the level dark gaze, and no hint of amusement to soften the hard lines of the mouth that had set her ablaze with kisses such a short while before.

She found her voice at last. 'You really think that is why—'

'Of course,' Vassos interrupted coldly. 'What other reason could there be for such a transformation? Or did you think I would share your naïveté and assume your surrender was genuine and without strings?' He shook his head almost grimly. 'You misjudge me, *pedhi mou*.'

And you, she thought, misjudge me. Completely. Because I gave you my heart as well as my body just now. God knows, I didn't expect love in return, but if you'd spoken just one word of kindness my soul would have followed and I'd have been yours for ever.

There were tears, thick and painful in her chest and burning her throat, but she would not weep in front of him in case he thought it was just another ploy. Another trick to have her way over Eleni.

She said, her voice shaking a little, 'Yes, *kyrie*. It seems that I have made a mistake. But it will never happen again.'

It was torture having to leave the bed, naked under his sardonic gaze, in order to retrieve her shawl, but she did it, wrapping herself closely in its folds with hands that trembled, then walking to the door without looking back.

She managed to regain her room before she began to cry, throwing herself across the bed, and stifling her sobs in her pillow.

And when the first storm had subsided she got up stiffly and went to the bathroom, standing under the warm torrent of the shower, letting it wash away all trace of anything and everything that had happened that night.

Wishing at the same time that it was possible to remove the memories and the regrets as easily as the tearstains.

I should have known, she thought wearily as she dried herself. Should have realised what Vassos would think when I just—turned up in his bedroom like that. Except, of course, I wasn't thinking, because I totally forgot to use any reason and let myself be carried away by the force of my emotions. By my need for him.

I was stupid—*stupid*—and now that it's all gone wrong I have no one to blame but myself.

But, dear God, I wanted him so badly. Wanted to know at last what it was to be a woman. His woman. And to give him everything.

Instead, she now had to come to terms with the inescapable fact that becoming his sexual partner for a brief while did not make her into any kind of woman, she thought bitterly, and it never would.

She'd proved nothing except that she was still a child—a pathetic child, like poor little Eleni, hoping each day for a love that would never be offered. And having to wake each morning to the sombre reality of disappointment.

She chose a clean nightdress, straightened the disordered bed, and crept under the covering sheet to lie wakeful and wretched, her awakened body restless. And it was not until dawn streaked the sky that she finally fell into an uneasy sleep.

It was late when she awoke, and as she sat up pushing her hair out of her eyes, she saw the bedroom door open and Hara appear almost as if she'd received some signal.

'Kyrios Vassos says to let you sleep,' she announced. 'He has important visitors from mainland, talking business this morning. I bring you breakfast here.'

Presumably because he doesn't want my presence known, Joanna thought bleakly. Though I'm sure the fact he has a mistress will come as no surprise to any of his guests.

'And am I to stay here in my room until the business is concluded?' she asked tautly, as she drank her orange juice and spread apricot jam on a warm roll.

Hara looked shocked. 'By no means, *thespinis*. Kyrios Vassos suggests you spend the day by the pool. He will join you later when other men leave.'

Joanna poured some coffee. She said woodenly, 'Just as he wishes,' and saw the fleeting look of relief on the older woman's face.

But while he's safely occupied with his talks, she thought, I have some business of my own to conduct. Because I refuse to just vanish from Eleni's life, no matter whose child she may be. It would be too cruel. So, whatever he says, I will see her again, even if it is only to say goodbye.

And if I'm simply justifying everything he said to me last night—so be it. He would expect no better.

Her breakfast finished, she dressed in brief candy-striped shorts and a matching halter-top in blue and white, and set off with her book, sunglasses and tanning oil for the pool, where a lounger had already been placed for her under the shade of a parasol.

Making sure I obey orders and keep out of harm's way, she

thought wryly. And for the first hour she did exactly that, although it would be unwise to wait too long before she departed on her mission, she decided, getting up from her lounger.

She deliberately uncapped her sun oil, and left her book lying casually open on the lounger, as if she only expected to be gone for a few moments, then made her way to the far side of the pool area and through a gap in the hibiscus hedge.

There was no one about, the air hot and still, apart from the drone of insects. None of the security men was visible, not even the obnoxious Yanni, so presumably everyone's attention was firmly focussed on the meeting inside the villa.

Besides, she thought, Vassos would no doubt consider that his word was law, and she would not dare to flout it.

Well, he was wrong about me last night, she told herself defiantly, fighting down the hurt that the memory of his words engendered. And he's wrong again today, although he'll never know that.

All the same, she found herself hurrying, trying to figure out what she would say when she arrived at the house—whether or not she would challenge Soula over her assertions. And why she'd made them.

But it's probably better not to ask, she thought. Instead keep it short and simple. Explain that I may be leaving Pellas quite soon, and won't have time for more visits. Because it could even be the truth.

Sighing, she rounded the final bend in the track and halted, staring with disbelief and sudden fear at the small crumpled pile of pink lying on the sandy ground straight ahead of her, with an overturned tricycle beside it.

For a second Joanna remained motionless, then she broke into a run, dropping on her knees beside Eleni.

The little girl's eyes were closed, she was breathing rapidly and her skin looked sallow. There was a bruise on her forehead, and even Joanna's untrained eyes could see that one small wrist looked an odd shape.

Her heart sank. Her first-aid experience was non-existent,

but she seemed to remember that fractures should be supported.

She threw her head back and yelled Soula's name as loudly as she could. There was no answer, and after a moment she shouted for her again, adding, '*Ela etho!* Come quickly.'

But there was still no reply.

Shut up in the house, no doubt, Joanna thought bitterly. Smoking and reading those picture magazines of hers. So God knows how long Eleni's been lying here.

But what on earth was the woman doing, allowing her to come out unsupervised? Because she could see what had happened. The tricycle's front wheel had hit a hidden root and Eleni had been thrown off.

Well, I'm not leaving her, she told herself with grim resolve. I won't let her come round and find she's alone and in pain. I can carry her to the house, where I shall a few things to say to Madam Soula. But first I have to do something about her wrist.

After a brief hesitation she stripped off her halter-neck, and managed to fashion it into a makeshift sling. As she gently moved Eleni's arm into position, the child moaned faintly and opened bewildered eyes.

'It's all right, Eleni *mou*,' Joanna said quietly, and stroked the tumbled dark hair as the little girl began to cry. 'I'll try not to hurt you, but we need to find help.'

She got to her feet, lifting the child carefully in her arms. It was only about fifty yards to the house, but when they reached it the gate was standing wide open, and the door was also ajar.

Soula must have realised Eleni was missing and gone to search, she told herself, as she deposited the whimpering child on a couch covered by a crocheted blanket, at the side of the room, and surrounded her with cushions.

Her first task was to find a teatowel or something similar and make a proper sling, so that she could retrieve her top. Even in front of Eleni she felt thoroughly self-conscious without it, and she had no wish for Soula to return and find her bared to the waist, as she could well imagine the kind of sniggering contempt she'd have to endure.

As she crossed to the small dresser to look for a towel she noticed that the votive light which burned in front of the icon had been allowed to go out—only to realise in the next instant that the icon itself wasn't there.

For a moment she hesitated, then made for the flight of steep wooden stairs in the corner. Eleni's room was tidy enough, but the larger room with the double bed was in complete disarray, its sheets rumpled and one pillow lying on the floor, with yet another overflowing ashtray on the night table.

As Joanna looked around her, wrinkling her nose at the stale atmosphere, she saw that the clothes cupboard was standing open and empty, as were the drawers in the adjoining chest.

My God, Joanna thought, drawing an appalled breath. She's not out searching at all. She's—gone. She knew I was coming, so she's abandoned Eleni and skipped.

And if I hadn't disobeyed Vassos the child might have been left to lie on the path, alone and injured, with potentially disastrous consequences.

Her nails curled into the palms of her hands. 'The witch,' she said aloud, her voice shaking. 'The evil, disgusting, *bloody* witch!'

She heard a little wail from the room below, and ran for the stairs.

'It's all right, darling,' she called. 'I'm coming.'

'So I see,' said Vassos.

He stood in the open doorway, dark against the brightness of the sun, his hands on his hips, his face a mask of anger carved from granite. He was wearing dark pants and a white shirt, and his wide silk tie was pulled loose.

Joanna halted at the foot of the stairs, her hands lifting to cover her bare breasts in an instinctive gesture of modesty. As if, she thought with a pang, there was any part of her he had not seen—or touched—or kissed.

She said, 'Oh, Vassos, I'm so thankful that you're here.'

'Are you?' His mouth curled into a smile that was grim and derisive at the same time. He looked past her at the stairway. 'Who is up there?' His tone was politely enquiring.

She stared at him. 'Are you mad? What are you talking about? There's no one.'

'I am expected to believe that?' He took a step forward. 'Just as you tried to persuade me you came here each day to visit a child who is nothing to you?' He shook his head slowly, his eyes going over her. 'I think not. So, I ask you again, Joanna, who have you just left in the bedroom?'

'Not a soul. The house is empty. See for yourself, if you want.' Her voice shook a little. 'Soula's left, and taken all her things. I only discovered it when I came back here with Eleni. She was in the grove, you see, and I found her. She's had an accident and broken her arm, so I had to use my top to make a sling for her,' she added, glancing down at herself and biting her lip.

'I saw the icon was missing, and went to check upstairs. I found that Soula had—gone—vanished—and if I hadn't come today Eleni would have been totally alone, because no one else ever comes here. God knows what might have happened to her. She's only a baby,' she went on, her voice cracking. 'A baby who desperately needs to see a doctor, while you stand there making—ludicrous accusations.'

She saw him turn, as if aware for the first time of the child in her nest of pillows.

He walked over to the couch and bent to look at the small arm in its makeshift support, and Joanna heard him say something quiet and savage under his breath.

'How did this happen?' he demanded.

'She fell off her tricycle. She bumped her head, too.'

'Yes.' He straightened, discarding his tie, then stripping off his shirt. He tossed it to Joanna. 'Cover yourself,' he directed brusquely.

'Oh, what does it matter?'

'It matters to me,' he said. 'We have to return to the villa, and I do not choose that any man but myself should see you even half-naked.'

The crisp fabric was still warm from his body, and she was aware of the scent of the cologne he used as she slipped her arms into the sleeves and fumbled the buttons into their holes.

'What's going to happen?' she asked, as Vassos bent and lifted the child into his arms with infinite care.

'She shall be taken to Thaliki. There is a hospital there. It is small but efficient, and she will receive excellent treatment.'

'And—afterwards?' Joanna watched him carry Eleni to the door. Look at her, she begged silently. Oh, my darling, look at her and see what I saw—please.

'Decisions will have to be made,' he returned curtly. 'Also Soula must be found. Wherever she is hiding,' he added ominously. 'She may have abandoned her charge, but there is no way that she can have left the island.'

She had to trot to keep up with his long stride. 'Why did you come here? I thought you were in a meeting.'

'It ended much sooner than I expected,' he responded bleakly. 'And in agreement, which I also did not anticipate. Once my colleagues had departed, I looked for you. When you could not be found, I guessed where you must be.'

'I had to do it,' she said in a low voice. 'You must understand that. And Soula must have known that, too.'

'It was a risk she had no right to take,' he said harshly.

After that there was silence between them until they reached the villa, where Andonis met them with an appalled look at the small crying burden in his employer's arms, then burst into a flood of agitated Greek.

Vassos listened, his head bent, his mouth hardening.

He turned to Joanna. 'Soula may have left Pellas after all,' he said harshly. 'The *caique* I use for night fishing has also disappeared, and so, it seems, has Yanni, one of the security men.' He paused. 'Did you ever see them together?'

Joanna bit her lip. 'No, but she was often missing in the afternoons.'

He said something under his breath. 'Then Hara will tend the child until Stavros returns with the launch and she can be taken to hospital.' His tone was brusque. 'There is nothing more for you to do.'

Joanna faced him, chin lifted defiantly. 'On the contrary, *kyrie*,' she said crisply. 'I shall go to the hospital with her. She's frightened and in pain, and she needs one familiar face around. Someone who actually cares about her.' She paused. 'And—in case you've forgotten—her name is Eleni.'

'This is not your concern—' he began, but she interrupted him fiercely.

'So you've told me, but I've just made it so. I'm going to my room to put on some proper clothes, so bring her there to me, please.'

She walked past Andonis, who looked as if he'd been pole-axed, and made for the stairs, aware that Vassos was staring after her.

In her room, she dragged off his shirt, wrenching open the buttons with such force that she sent several of them skittering across the floor.

'To hell with it,' she muttered, sending the shirt to join them. 'He'll have a thousand others to take its place.'

She removed her shorts, replacing them with a green dress, full-skirted and short-sleeved, grabbed at random from the wardrobe.

She was dragging a comb through her hair when Vassos knocked abruptly and entered with Eleni, crying loudly and fretfully now in his arms, and an anxious Hara close behind.

'Stavros has been contacted by radio,' he said. 'He will be here very soon.' He paused. 'The *caique* has been seen drifting, perhaps with engine trouble, by some fishermen.'

She said stonily, 'I wouldn't care if it had blown up.' She

sat down on the chair by the window. 'Give Eleni to me, please.'

He said more gently, 'Let Hara take her, Joanna *mou*.'

'No.' She shook her head. 'I began this. So I'll look after her while she's here. After all, you can't pretend that anyone here wants her, not when you all did your best to keep us apart.' She took the sobbing child gently on her lap, looking down at the creased and dirty pink dress.

'And, whatever you decide for her, *kyrie,* she'll need new clothes,' she added. 'Normal things, too. Not more of these awful party frocks that Soula picked for her. Because her life's going to be no party.'

'Joanna.' His voice was quiet. 'Let us talk about this.'

'And say what? That I shouldn't have interfered? I think it's already been said.'

She bent her head. 'And I suppose I have to agree with you. If I hadn't—intervened as I did, Soula would never have dared to go off like this and Eleni wouldn't have been put in danger.' She paused. 'Also you wouldn't have been forced to remember your—your marriage and its unhappiness. Is that what you want to hear?'

'No,' he said. 'But why should you believe me?' He turned and left the room, signalling to Hara to accompany him.

Joanna leaned back, careful not to jolt Eleni's injured arm. She felt very tired suddenly, with the beginnings of a headache. But that was nothing compared with the desolation inside her.

I wanted to help, she thought wretchedly, but instead I've simply made everything much worse. Because this accident will have to be explained somehow, and that will trigger all the problems that Vassos most wants to avoid.

And now, she realised, to add to her feelings of guilt, the child's warm body was curling trustingly into hers, and her sobs were beginning to subside a little.

'Try and sleep, darling,' Joanna said softly as Eleni's thumb stole to her mouth and her eyelids drooped. 'The doctor will stop your poor arm aching very soon.' And quietly she began to sing, '"There were ten green bottles, hanging on the wall…"'

She was over halfway through the song, deliberately allowing her voice to sink lower, watching Eleni's small face relax and her breathing steady and deepen, when she felt her own skin begin to tingle as if she was being watched. Knowing that there was only one person in the world who could trigger that particular reaction.

But when, at last, she ventured to glance towards the doorway it was empty. I must have been imagining things, she told herself with an inward sigh. Or just indulging in some wishful thinking.

And her song was finished, and she was sitting cradling the sleeping child, prey to her unhappy thoughts, well before Hara came to tell her that Stavros and the launch had returned and it was time to go.

The hospital on Thaliki might not be large, but Joanna saw at once that it was scrupulously clean and efficiently run, as Vassos had said.

Dr Deroulos, who came to take charge of Eleni, was a short man, his hair and beard grizzled, his eyes calm and kind, as Joanna haltingly explained there had been an accident with a tricycle.

'These things happen with small children,' was his comment. He gave Joanna a thoughtful look. 'And you, *thespinis?* Who are you?'

She said quietly, 'I'm Eleni's temporary nanny,' and did not look at Vassos, standing beside her like a statue.

Eleni was borne away to have her arm set and plastered, and to be checked for any signs of concussion after the bump on her head.

Joanna and Vassos retired to a small, square waiting room, silently taking chairs on its opposite sides. After a while, Joanna ventured to steal a look at him from under her lashes, and saw that his face was set like stone, and that he was staring into space with eyes that seemed to see nothing.

After half an hour had passed, with nothing being said on either side, they were joined by Stavros. Vassos listened to his murmured words, then rose, looking across at Joanna.

'The police have boarded the *caique* and arrested Yanni and Soula,' he said brusquely. 'I am required to help deal with this matter, and I must also arrange for Kostas, who goes fishing with me at night to collect the boat. There will be statements. Maybe a question of charges.' He paused. 'Will you be all right—alone here?'

'Yes,' she said. 'Of course.'

And being alone is something I shall have to get used to.

She paused. 'Did you say you go fishing at night?'

He paused at the door, brows lifting. 'Sometimes,' he said. 'If I find I cannot sleep. Why do you ask?'

'It just seems—an odd thing to do,' Joanna returned, thinking of all the times his footsteps had passed her door in the darkness.

'But then,' he said softly. 'So many other strange things seem to be happening in my life. *Herete andio,* Joanna.' And he went.

Over an hour had passed before Dr Deroulos returned with the news that the fracture had been reduced, the bump on Eleni's head was just what it seemed and nothing more serious, and the little girl would soon recover from the anaesthetic she'd been given while her arm received attention.

'Oh, thank heavens.' Joanna sank back on her chair. 'I've been so worried.'

'You must not blame yourself, *thespinis*,' he told her kindly. 'And nor, I am sure, does Kyrios Gordanis. A healthy child must be allowed to run and play. And little Eleni, in spite of her unpromising beginning, is now fit and well. Her father must rejoice to see it.' He glanced round. 'He has gone somewhere?'

'To the police station, I think,' Joanna said awkwardly. 'There's been a—problem with the previous nanny.'

'*Po, po, po,* he should marry again,' the doctor said. 'Provide his daughter with a mother's care. After all a young, virile man cannot be expected to grieve for ever.' He frowned a little. 'I think it haunts him still that he was not present at the birth or at his wife's side when she so sadly died. But with a premature child like Eleni these things are not always possible to arrange. I just thank the good God that, after a struggle, we were able to save her for him, so he did not have a double tragedy to bear.'

Joanna stared at him. 'You say Eleni was—premature?' She shook her head. 'I—I didn't know that.' She hesitated. 'How early was she?'

'Barely seven months.' He sighed. 'And so tiny—so fragile. For days she hovered between life and death.'

Joanna said urgently, 'Did Vassos—Kyrios Gordanis, I mean—know this? How delicate Eleni was—and why?'

'He was in shock after the death of Kyria Ariadne, *thespinis.* Like a man living through a nightmare. My colleague Dr Christaphis decided it would be wrong to burden him with the possibility of further sadness.'

He smiled suddenly. 'And it did not happen. The Holy Virgin had the child in her protection and she was spared, to become healthy and happy.' He spread his hands. 'So what was said or not said at the time surely cannot matter. Not now. Not any more.'

'On the contrary,' Joanna said softly, her heart lifting. 'I think it could matter very much, Dr Deroulos. Very much indeed.'

CHAPTER THIRTEEN

IT WAS another hour before Vassos returned.

Joanna had spent the time on tenterhooks, mentally rehearsing what she wanted to say. What he so desperately needed to know.

But when he finally appeared in the waiting room doorway, she took one look at his exhausted eyes, and the greyish tinge to his skin as he halted, putting out a hand as if to steady himself against the doorframe, then jumped to her feet, spilling the remains of the coffee they'd brought her down her skirt.

All the careful words were forgotten. She said, 'Vassos—about Eleni. There's something I must tell you.'

He lifted a silencing finger. 'I already know what you are going to say, Joanna. I have heard the whole story from Soula Karadis, no doubt in the vain hope that the truth would make me grateful enough to spare her.'

His voice was almost toneless. 'It would seem that my late wife hated me even more than I thought possible. She did have a lover before our marriage—but her pregnancy by him was just a figment of her imagination, invented to drive me away. Which means that Eleni is indeed my daughter, born from the one moment of intimacy in our marriage. But brought into the world much too soon, when her mother decided to throw herself down a flight of steps to rob me of the son she believed she was carrying. Something else I did not know until now.'

He added harshly, 'It is almost beyond belief. Yet, having known Ariadne, even briefly, I find I can—and do—believe it.'

He looked at her. 'And you have heard—what?'

'Nothing like that,' she denied huskily. 'Just that Eleni was born at least two months premature, and they were afraid she wouldn't survive.' She ran the tip of her tongue round her dry lips. 'But no one told you at the time because it was felt you had enough to bear with your—grief for your wife.'

'Ironic, is it not?' His smile was a slash of pain. 'And yet I think I did experience an element of grief, if only for a young life cut off so suddenly and so harshly. Guilt, too,' he added bitterly, 'that I did not realise just how much she resented our proposed marriage and stop it for both our sakes while I had the chance. Although it is doubtful if that would have kept her alive.

'But she had her revenge.' His voice thickened. 'She died leaving me with the hideous belief that my daughter was another man's child. Someone I could not even bear to look at. And by doing so Ariadne robbed me of the right to love her—to enjoy her babyhood and watch her grow.' His voice sank to a whisper. 'And I might never have known. Never...'

'But you do know now,' Joanna said fiercely. 'So everything can change. That's what really matters.' She looked away from him, her throat tightening, longing to go to him and feel his arms close around her. But instead forcing herself to remain where she was. 'It—it's all that can matter.'

'Except,' he said, 'that I owe this knowledge to you. If you had not gone to the house today...' He closed his eyes. 'I do not want to think what might have happened.'

'Then think of something else,' she said. 'Like being beside Eleni's bedside when she wakes up next time.' She paused, trying to smile. 'I hope she'll be more welcoming for you. She was cross and a little nauseous when she came round from the anaesthetic, and demanded to be sung to.'

'Ah,' Vassos said quietly. 'That same song I first heard in the gardens at the St Gregoire?'

She stared at him. 'You—heard me?'

'I heard a baby crying,' he said. 'And a girl singing a lullaby. So, I stood and listened for a while, and wondered if the singer was as lovely as her voice. I did not know, of course—how could I?—that she was the beauty I had seen earlier from the deck of *Persephone,* or the girl I planned to meet later that night across a poker table.'

He drew a deep breath. 'And today I heard you comforting a sick child with the same melody. And for a moment I could not believe it.' He paused. 'Why were you there in the garden that night?'

She looked down at the floor. 'I was just babysitting for a couple I'd met.' She found a resolute smile from somewhere. 'And I really liked taking care of Matthew, so I've decided I shall train to look after children professionally one day.'

One day when I'm back in England, and need to find a life for myself—a life that you are no longer a part of. When other people's children may be all I can hope for...

He was frowning. 'Is that why you told Deroulos that you were Eleni's nanny?'

'I had to think of some reason for being here.' She flushed a little. 'After all, I could hardly say I was your mistress.'

'No,' he said, his mouth twisting. 'Perhaps, for the time being, the fiction that you are Eleni's nursemaid will serve us better, *pedhi mou.*'

And maybe, she whispered silently, for the sake of my aching heart, it might be better—easier—if fiction becomes fact. If I become your employee instead of your pillow friend from now on—until you send me away.

As they walked along the passage towards the small private room where Eleni was installed, Dr Deroulos was coming to meet them.

'Your daughter is awake, Kyrios Gordanis.' He turned a

kindly smile on Joanna. 'And once again demanding you, *thespinis.*'

Joanna halted. She said quietly, 'I think she should spend some time alone with her father now.' She indicated her coffee-stained skirt. 'Maybe I could go somewhere and clean my dress?'

'But of course. It will be a pleasure.' He signalled to a female orderly, and Joanna was whisked off to a gleaming washroom and supplied with a sponge and towels for a strictly rudimentary rescue job.

But what did a ruined dress matter? she asked herself bleakly, surveying her reflection in the mirror, when it was her life that was about to fall apart?

Yes, Vassos was grateful to her, but she did not want him to turn to her in gratitude, because her intervention had restored his child to him. She needed far more from him than that.

Now, when it was too late, she wanted the tender, passionate lover whom she'd so signally rejected so many times. Wanted to offer him again all the warmth and the ardent, generous desire he'd kindled in her. And to prove to him, beyond all doubt, that her gift to him came from the heart, and without strings.

I love him, she thought painfully, and I always will, but I can't stay with him, longing all the time for something he can never give. Knowing I have nothing to hope for except his transient desire. And even that will end.

He took me for all the wrong reasons, at a time when his bed and his life were both empty and he needed entertainment. Distraction.

But now the circumstances have changed. He has a daughter to love, who will adore him in return. And one day he'll remarry, this time to a girl who will love him and give Eleni brothers and sisters. And then that barren house will come alive again at last.

At which time, please God, I shall be far away.

When she finally emerged from the washroom, she turned

initially to go back to the waiting room, then after a moment's hesitation made her way quietly along the passage to the ward.

The door was open and she could see Vassos kneeling beside the bed, Eleni's small hand clasped in his, and his head was bent as if he was crying—or praying.

Whichever it was, Joanna thought, her heart twisting as tears stung her eyes, her presence would only be an intrusion. And she stole silently away.

She had herself strictly under control when he eventually returned to the waiting room.

'How is she?' she asked brightly.

'Well, and asking for almond biscuits.' He paused. 'However, the doctor suggests that she remain here overnight so that he can make sure there are no after-effects from all the shocks she has suffered today.' His smile was wry. 'I suspect I am not the least of them.'

Joanna bit her lip. 'Ever since she's been able to understand what was being said to her, she's been told, "Papa will come." And now you have done.'

'And now Papa will stay,' he said softly. 'And we will take her home in the morning.'

Joanna glanced uncertainly at the waiting room chairs. 'You mean—spend the night here?'

'No.' His tone was faintly brusque. 'Thaliki has a hotel—the Poseidon. They will have a room for us.'

'But we'll need two,' she said. 'One for you—and another for Eleni's nanny.'

There was an odd silence, then he said, 'Is that truly what you wish? To spend this night apart from me?'

'Yes, or I wouldn't have said it.' She lifted her chin, fighting her inner misery. 'You should know that by now.'

'At times like this I feel as if I know nothing about you, Joanna *mou*,' he said harshly. 'Nothing at all.' He paused. 'And now Eleni is waiting to say goodnight to you. I warn you, she may ask for another song. I hope she will not also be disappointed.'

And he walked out into the corridor, leaving her to follow.

It had been, Joanna thought, as she lay in bed, staring at the ceiling, the longest two weeks of her life. And here she was, faced with yet another sunlit morning. Which, somehow, she would have to survive.

At least in the daytime she could keep busy, looking after Eleni who'd adapted with astonishing speed to her new circumstances, even with a plaster on her arm. Proving, Joanna mused, just how resilient children could be.

And for this, admittedly, Vassos deserved much of the credit, approaching his new role as a father with patience, humour and an element of firmness. Above all spending unstinted time with her, overcoming her initial shyness and, in return, receiving his daughter's unquestioning adoration.

But, rather to Joanna's concern, Eleni was inclined to treat her in much the same way, which she feared might lead to problems when a real nanny was eventually appointed in her place.

Vassos had made several flying visits to Athens over the past fortnight, presumably to interview potential candidates, but seemed to have made no final choice.

In fact, Joanna had started to wonder if he might choose a British nanny, as he also appeared to be teaching Eleni to use English as well as Greek names for the things she saw around her, but when she'd ventured to ask him, on one of the few occasions when they'd been briefly alone, he'd retorted that English was the international language of commerce throughout the world and Eleni, as an adult, might well need to speak it fluently.

Which did not sound, she thought unhappily, as if he ever expected to have a son to succeed him.

Apart from that, relations between them were studiedly

formal. And when Eleni was not around he seemed quiet and preoccupied, as if in another less sunlit world.

She'd become a member of his staff, she thought painfully. Just as she'd asked. Except that she'd never dreamed how difficult it would be to make such a transition. To share a roof with him, but nothing else.

In the daytime she could cope. Just. But the nights were a very different matter.

She was no longer occupying her former room but, at her own suggestion, had moved to one adjoining Eleni's new nursery, in case the little girl needed anything in the night.

Hara had indicated, clearly bewildered at this turn of events, that a couple of the maids could take over Eleni's night-time supervision, the entire household having become her devoted slaves from the moment the child entered the villa, but Joanna had refused with determination, saying that the little girl would prefer to see a familiar face if she woke.

In fact Eleni was a sound sleeper, so Joanna was rarely disturbed in this way, but that made little difference to the wreckage of her own sleep patterns. Heartache and loneliness were her regular companions during long and restless vigils.

And when she did sleep her dreams were erotic fantasies that woke her, gasping, her body on fire, her hands reaching for him and finding emptiness.

She was losing weight, and the shadows beneath her eyes were deepening into violet pools.

I'm fretting, she told herself wryly. And, heaven help me, it shows. So, perhaps it's a good thing that Vassos rarely looks at me these days.

She flung back the sheet and left the bed, taking a quick shower before dressing in a midi-skirt, in shades of rust and gold, topped with a sleeveless cream shirt. Her hair she brushed back and secured at the nape of her neck with an elastic band.

Then she went next door to rouse Eleni, wash and dress her, then take her down to breakfast on the terrace.

Vassos rose from the table at their approach. *'Kalimera,'* he said softly, inclining his head to Joanna before going down on his haunches to greet Eleni with a kiss as she ran to him.

Joanna sat down, busying herself with buttering a slice of bread, adding honey, and pouring a glass of milk for Eleni. She applauded, smiling, as the little girl, prompted by Vassos, pointed to each item in turn and said its English name, before collapsing in giggles.

As Joanna poured her own coffee, and set down the pot, Vassos said abruptly, 'Joanna, I must tell you that Stavros has gone to Thaliki to bring back Eleni's new nursemaid. My cousin Maria has found a girl who has worked with English families in Athens, so can speak your language well. Her name is Mitsa, which is short for Artemis, and she comes highly recommended.'

He paused. 'I have also made immediate arrangements for your departure, which I hope will please you. When breakfast is over, I suggest that you pack.'

Joanna stared at him, her whole being suddenly numb. She said in a voice she didn't recognise, 'So soon?' *And just that brief dismissal as if there had been nothing between us? Nothing...*

'I feel it would be best,' he said. 'Before Eleni becomes too dependent on you.'

Her mouth was dry. 'Yes,' she said. 'I suppose that is—a danger. And I—I wouldn't want to do anything to hurt her.'

His faint smile did not reach his eyes. 'No,' he said. 'That is one thing I can be sure of. And in that she has been fortunate indeed.'

She forced herself to drink her coffee and eat a roll with black cherry jam, in spite of the desperate churning of her stomach.

I'm going, she thought. I'll never see him again, and I don't know how I can bear it. Especially when he clearly can't wait to be rid of me.

She supposed she should ask about her travel plans—or at

least what UK airport she was destined for. She'd find Chris and Julie's address—ask them if they could put her up for a night or two while she tried to make some kind of rational decision about her future.

She pushed her chair back and rose. 'If you'll excuse me, I'll get ready. I'll only take the things I brought here with me, so it won't take long.'

He took a table napkin and wiped Eleni's sticky fingers. 'As you wish,' he said, after a long pause, adding, without looking up, 'Eleni will stay with me while you make your final preparations.'

When she reached her room, Hara had already brought the small case which had arrived on Pellas with her. It was open on the bed, displaying its meagre contents, the black crochet dress and the white boots on top of the other things.

'This is a day of much sadness, *thespinis*. Why do you go when you are needed here?'

'Someone called Mitsa will be looking after Eleni,' Joanna returned over-brightly. 'She'll be fine.'

'I do not speak of the child, Kyria Joanna, but her father. Who is to care for Kyrios Vassos if you do not?'

Joanna retrieved the black dress and its body stocking and began to change into them. Leaving, she thought, the way she'd arrived.

She said haltingly, 'Well, there's you—and Andonis. And Eleni herself, of course. And there are plenty of other women in the world—especially his world.' She tried to smile. 'He once told me that one girl is very like another.'

'*Po, po, po,*' Hara dismissed with a snort. 'That is when he knew nothing. Now he knows everything—and he suffers. You should stay,' she added coaxingly. 'Make him happy in bed. Give him more babies.'

Joanna shook her head. 'That isn't possible.' *Because it's the last thing he wants. He's made that clear.* 'I have another life in England,' she hurried on. 'And I need to get back to it.' *And somehow begin to heal…*

Hara snorted again and went off, muttering under her breath.

She was fastening her case when Stavros knocked at the door. 'Kyrios Gordanis requests you join him in the *saloni, thespinis*.'

He took the case from her hand, and followed her to the stairs. Joanna went down them, the heels of the white boots clicking, her head held high, feeling the thud of her heart against her ribcage.

'Please don't let him offer me money,' she whispered under her breath. 'Just my ticket home and no more. I need to get through this with my pride left, if nothing else.'

And knew just how deep, how painful and how endless 'nothing else' might well be.

Andonis was waiting to open the door of the *saloni* for her, and, taking a deep breath, Joanna walked into the room beyond and paused, looking across at Vassos, his face pale under its tan and strangely haggard, the dark eyes fixed on her with an aching intensity that struck her like a blow—because she recognised it. Shared it.

Joanna took one quick, involuntary step towards him, then stopped as another voice said her name, and she realised for the first time that they were not alone.

Incredulously, she whirled round in the direction of the speaker.

'Daddy?' Her voice cracked on the word. 'What are you doing here?'

'I've come to take you back where you belong, Joanna.' Denys Vernon crossed to where she was standing and kissed her awkwardly on the forehead. He was wearing a light-coloured suit with wide lapels and a flowered shirt open at the neck, all clearly expensive. His hair had been cut short on top, growing down into sideburns.

He looked sleek and prosperous, Joanna thought, but his eyes were restless and did not meet hers.

He added, tight-lipped, 'Mr Gordanis has finally decided he has no more use for you, and has summoned us to fetch you.'

Vassos said nothing, but turned away, walking over to the windows, his body taut, his hands clenching into fists at his sides.

'Us?' Joanna repeated without comprehension. She looked past her father at the sofa behind him, and her eyes widened as she recognised his companion. 'My God,' she said shakily. 'Mrs Van Dyne.'

'Mrs Vernon, if you don't mind, honey.' The older woman was her usual immaculate self in ice blue silk. 'Which is a surprise for you, I can see.' She shrugged. 'But you were news to me, too, especially as I knew back in France Denys had been passing you off as some kind of niece.'

Her eyes went disparagingly over Joanna's outfit. 'Well, your millionaire seems to have got you cheap, my dear, unless you have some serious jewellery packed away in that little hold-all. After all, he should pay for his pleasures, if that's what they were, of course. You're hardly the sophisticated type, but I presume he's still going to be generous with the severance cheque.'

She paused. 'Besides, there's always the additional question of compensation. Poor Denys, suffering the trauma of being robbed of his own child and in such a way. He may be scarred for life. Plus, it's cost us an arm and a leg getting here from the States, not to mention the inconvenience.' She rolled her eyes. 'That crazy little plane from Athens to that other island, then a boat trip, of all things.'

She glanced round her, lips pursed. 'But at least, having snatched you, Mr Gordanis has kept you here in this hideaway, instead of flaunting you round the world as his floozie. Maybe we can keep the whole thing under wraps and get you decently married off, after all.'

'Married?' Joanna repeated in bewilderment, her mind whirling under the torrent of words.

The elegant shoulders were shrugged. 'Well, you aren't

trained for anything, so Denys informs me. And you're short on qualifications, so you can't expect me to support you as well as him.' She sniffed. 'We daren't risk the top drawer, of course, but there are plenty of young lawyers and executives at the country club. It shouldn't be too much of a problem, especially when it's known you're my stepdaughter. Just as long as the newspapers don't get hold of what's been going on, which none of us want, I'm quite sure.'

She gave Joanna another disparaging look. 'A few trips to the beauty parlour and some better clothes will help, of course. We certainly don't wish to advertise that you're second-hand goods.'

She nodded briskly. 'So, when your father and Mr Gordanis have had their little chat about money, we can be getting back to civilisation, thank the Lord. And I want to make it quite clear that this—incident—is now permanently over, and we don't refer to it again. As far as the world's concerned, honey, you've been vacationing with friends.'

Joanna looked at the dark, unmoving figure by the window. The profile hewn out of stone. The rigid curl of his fists.

'Yes,' Denys joined in, his tone blustering, yet uneasy at the same time. 'My wife is quite right. You're going to pay for what you've done to my innocent girl. So don't think you can simply hand her back and get away with it.'

'No.' Vassos' voice was quiet and husky, with a note in it Joanna had never heard before. 'I have never thought that. And believe me, Kyrios Vernon, I will pay. Pay whatever you ask, and far more besides.'

Now he knows everything—and he suffers...

Hara's words were suddenly beating in Joanna's brain. And, as if a new sun had arisen above the eastern horizon, illumining her entire world, she realised what she had to do.

Lifting her chin, she said, coolly and clearly, 'I'm sorry to spoil all these careful arrangements, but I'm afraid it's not quite as simple as that. Because I have no intention of leaving. You see, I realised this morning that I'm going to have Mr Gordanis' baby, and that changes everything.'

There was a moment of stunned silence. Joanna was aware of Vassos swinging round from the window, his dark face incredulous.

'Are you crazy?' her stepmother demanded derisively. 'My God, I'll bet he has the known world littered with his bastards. One more won't make any difference, you little fool. He'll still dump you.'

She allowed her voice to become more coaxing. 'Look, honey, you can't be that far on. Nothing that a good gynaecologist can't sort out for you. Cut your losses and come away before the press finds out and goes to town on you. Look what poor Maria Callas went through.'

'Wait.' Vassos' voice cut across any further arguments she was about to marshal. He walked across to Joanna and took both her hands in his. He said gravely, 'You told me once, Joanna *mou,* that you had no wish to bear me a child. Something I have never forgotten. If you have now changed your mind, tell me why.'

She looked up at him, her heart twisting at the searching, agonised tenderness in his eyes. She said softly, 'I think you already know.'

'Yet I need to hear you say it.' His voice deepened. Became urgent. 'Or shall I speak first? Tell you what is in my heart too? *S'agapo, matia mou.* I love you.'

He lifted her hands almost reverently to his lips, kissing the soft palms. '*M'agapas,* Joanna? Can you love me, in spite of all the wrong I have done you? And will you stay with me and become my wife, and let us make each other happy for the rest of our lives?'

Her lips trembled into a smile. '*S'agapo,* Vassos *mou.* I love you so very much. And I'd marry you today if it was possible.'

For the first time in weeks his face relaxed into something approaching the familiar grin. 'I think it will take a little longer than that, *agapi mou*. But I also have no wish to wait. Nor any intention of doing so,' he added softly, his lips brushing her ear, making her whole body thrill to his touch, and its promise.

'Just hold it right there.' Nora Vernon was on her feet. 'I've heard of this before—girls falling in love with their kidnappers. So what's your thinking, Mr Greek Almighty? That it will be cheaper to fool her into believing you want her rather than paying us to take her off your hands? Well, forget it. A few sessions with a good therapist will stop that nonsense, and you can pay for those, too.'

She turned on her husband. 'Don't just stand there, Denys. She's your daughter! She's not thinking straight. You've got to do something.'

'Yes, Kyrios Vernon,' Vassos said harshly. 'Do something, indeed. For the first time in your life behave like a father and give my Joanna your blessing and your consent to our marriage. Because whatever you or this—woman of yours may say or do, I shall take your daughter as my wife to cherish always.

'And why did I have to send for you?' he added contemptuously. 'Why did you not seek me out long ago and force me to give her up, at gunpoint if necessary, after what I had done? I traced you without difficulty. Why could you not find me? What excuse do you have?'

He drew a deep unsteady breath. 'Because I, too, have a daughter, *kyrie,* and I know now that if a man ever took her from me in such a way, I would find him and kill him. It has made me realise exactly the wrong I have done. Therefore I decided I must let Joanna go from me, even though I would be tearing the heart out of my body, because it might be my only hope of putting things right between us. But you—you never lifted a finger to rescue her,' he went on, eyes blazing remorselessly at the man who stood, head bent, in front of him. 'You left her to endure whatever treatment I chose to inflict on her while you saved yourself.

'I am not sure you would be here now if your wife had not believed you could make "a fast buck", as I believe the saying is. Cash in on your child's supposed disgrace at my hands.' He shook his head. 'Even so, I told myself if I restored her to you it would be a step towards forgiveness, and a new beginning for us both, even if I did not deserve such happiness.'

He drew Joanna close, his arm strong around her slender waist, his voice quiet and sure. 'Because—unlike you—I would have come to the other ends of the earth to find her again, and, if God was good, to teach her to love me. To persuade her that my life was hers.'

His clasp tightened a little. 'Our need for each other did not flower slowly and gently from trust and liking, as it should have done—I wish with all my soul it had happened that way— but it is no less real. And, no matter how it began, it is ending well. She is my woman, I am her man, and nothing can change that.'

He added curtly, 'You will be notified when the arrangements for our wedding have been made, so that you may attend if you wish to do so. And, in time, you will be free to visit your grandchildren.'

'Denys?' His wife's face was cold with fury as she got to her feet. 'Are you going to stand that kind of talk from this— barbarian? Let him dictate to you?'

There was a silence, then Denys Vernon said tiredly, 'What has he said that isn't the truth? Of course I should have come to fetch her. I wanted to, Nora, as you well know. Asked for your help. But you wouldn't allow it. Not until now—when you thought there might be money to be made. He's right about that, too, heaven help us.'

He straightened sagging shoulders. 'But I shall come to the wedding, and this time give my daughter away in the true and proper sense. That is if she can forgive me for the part I've played in all this.' He added heavily, 'You, Nora, will please yourself, as you always do.'

As she parted her lips to speak, her skin mottled with anger, he raised a silencing hand. 'And before you tell me again that you took me from the gutter, I know it. I only wish I could feel more grateful.' He took her arm. 'Now, let's leave while there's still a way back for us.'

Joanna detached herself gently from Vassos' embrace and went to him.

'Daddy.' She put a hand on his sleeve. 'There'll always be a way back. I discovered that a little while ago in this room, just when I thought I'd lost everything.' She added more strongly, 'And the past is exactly that. It's over. So I'd love you to give me away.'

He said unsteadily, 'Bless you for that, my darling. I've been so terribly ashamed—about everything.' He paused. 'I'll be waiting to hear from you. From both of you.' He took her in his arms and held her for a long moment while his wife, stony-faced, walked to the door.

Then he followed her, as Joanna watched, tears stinging her eyes.

Vassos said gently, *'Agapi mou,'* and, gulping, she flew back to his arms. He lifted her and carried her to a sofa, settling her on his lap, before taking the elastic band from her hair and combing the shining strands loose with fingers that shook a little.

She said in a whisper, 'Were you really going to send me away?'

'Only so that I could come and find you, my precious one. As I should have done that day when we first looked at each other. As I almost did,' he added in a low voice. 'Until I told myself I was there for revenge, not to fall in love. Then, that night, when I realised who you were, I cursed the Fates for playing me such a trick. For making you a girl I could never have as my own. Only to find, when I took you, that I had been wrong—about you—about everything—and that somehow I must atone for what I had done. I thought—I hoped—that when we were truly lovers things might change. That I could persuade you to enjoy being in my arms. Make you want to stay for ever. But it did not happen, and I knew I had only myself to blame. That I had hurt you, repelled you.'

'You think I didn't want you?' Joanna played with one of the buttons on his shirt. 'Oh, Vassos, I did. Almost from the beginning, even though I wouldn't admit it.' She swallowed. 'After I'd left you that first night, I couldn't sleep for thinking of you, so I decided to go back to your room.'

He turned her face up to his. 'Then why did you not do so, my sweet one?'

'Because you decided to go fishing.' Her mouth trembled into a smile. 'I watched you leave. And after that—you were so different. I didn't know how to get near you.'

'One smile, *agapi mou,* one touch of your hand would have been enough,' he said unsteadily. 'I was dying for you. Desperate to love you as you deserved. But scared to show you in case you turned away for ever.'

He paused. 'I went to Athens to think. I feared you would always regard Pellas—and this house—as a prison, and that if there was to be any hope for us it would have to begin elsewhere. Even when you gave yourself to me at last, I could not believe that you really wanted me. I thought you were simply using my need for you for your own purpose, and I was bitter. Then, when I heard the truth about Eleni, I knew I had to begin my atonement by returning you to your father. That there could be no other way.'

He gave a faint groan. 'I was trying so hard to behave well, but when they came and I heard his wife—how she spoke to you—what she was planning—I knew I could not let you go. I would beg you on my knees to stay with me.'

She kissed him softly. 'Except I didn't give you the chance.'

'No, *agapi mou.* Instead you gave me the whole world.' He paused. 'Is there really to be a baby? I ask because it has occurred to me that when you came to me at last I forgot to be careful.'

Joanna smiled into his eyes, her hand stroking his cheek

'No, darling, I'm not pregnant. Not yet. What I said just now was a promise for the future, not a statement of fact. Although I think Eleni would like to have a little brother or sister, don't you?'

'Yes, my dearest one.' Vassos drew her closer. 'But first, and more importantly, I want to have a wife.'

'But until you're married,' she whispered, 'won't you still need a pillow friend?'

'A pillow friend.' He kissed her. 'A companion.' He kissed her again.

'And a sweetheart for the whole of my life. And do you know something, *agapi mou?*' he murmured against her lips. 'By some miracle they are all called—Joanna.'

Harlequin *Presents*

Coming Next Month

from **Harlequin Presents® EXTRA.** Available May 10, 2011.

#149 BREAKING THE SHEIKH'S RULES
Abby Green
Kings of the Desert

#150 THE INHERITED BRIDE
Maisey Yates
Kings of the Desert

#151 HER BAD, BAD BOSS
Nicola Marsh
In Bed with the Boss

#152 THE ROGUE WEDDING GUEST
Ally Blake
In Bed with the Boss

Coming Next Month

from **Harlequin Presents®.** Available May 31, 2011.

#2993 FOR DUTY'S SAKE
Lucy Monroe

#2994 TAMING THE LAST ST. CLAIRE
Carole Mortimer
The Scandalous St. Claires

#2995 THE FORBIDDEN WIFE
Sharon Kendrick
The Powerful and the Pure

#2996 ONE LAST NIGHT
Melanie Milburne
The Sabbatini Brothers

#2997 THE SECRET SHE CAN'T HIDE
India Grey

#2998 THE HEIR FROM NOWHERE
Trish Morey

Visit www.HarlequinInsideRomance.com
for more information on upcoming titles!

REQUEST YOUR
FREE BOOKS!

◆ Harlequin *Presents*®

(PASSION GUARANTEED SEDUCTION)

2 FREE NOVELS PLUS
2 FREE GIFTS!

YES! Please send me 2 FREE Harlequin Presents® novels and my 2 FREE gifts (gifts are worth about $10). After receiving them, if I don't wish to receive any more books, I can return the shipping statement marked "cancel." If I don't cancel, I will receive 6 brand-new novels every month and be billed just $4.05 per book in the U.S. or $4.74 per book in Canada. That's a saving of at least 15% off the cover price! It's quite a bargain! Shipping and handling is just 50¢ per book in the U.S. and 75¢ per book in Canada.* I understand that accepting the 2 free books and gifts places me under no obligation to buy anything. I can always return a shipment and cancel at any time. Even if I never buy another book, the two free books and gifts are mine to keep forever.

106/306 HDN FC55

Name   (PLEASE PRINT)

Address   Apt. #

City   State/Prov.   Zip/Postal Code

Signature (if under 18, a parent or guardian must sign)

Mail to the **Reader Service:**
IN U.S.A.: P.O. Box 1867, Buffalo, NY 14240-1867
IN CANADA: P.O. Box 609, Fort Erie, Ontario L2A 5X3

Not valid for current subscribers to Harlequin Presents books.

**Are you a current subscriber to Harlequin Presents books
and want to receive the larger-print edition?
Call 1-800-873-8635 or visit www.ReaderService.com.**

* Terms and prices subject to change without notice. Prices do not include applicable taxes. Sales tax applicable in N.Y. Canadian residents will be charged applicable taxes. Offer not valid in Quebec. This offer is limited to one order per household. All orders subject to credit approval. Credit or debit balances in a customer's account(s) may be offset by any other outstanding balance owed by or to the customer. Please allow 4 to 6 weeks for delivery. Offer available while quantities last.

Your Privacy—The Reader Service is committed to protecting your privacy. Our Privacy Policy is available online at www.ReaderService.com or upon request from the Reader Service.

We make a portion of our mailing list available to reputable third parties that offer products we believe may interest you. If you prefer that we not exchange your name with third parties, or if you wish to clarify or modify your communication preferences, please visit us at www.ReaderService.com/consumerschoice or write to us at Reader Service Preference Service, P.O. Box 9062, Buffalo, NY 14269. Include your complete name and address.

Harlequin® Blaze™ brings you
New York Times *and* USA TODAY *bestselling author*
Vicki Lewis Thompson with three new steamy titles
from the bestselling miniseries SONS OF CHANCE

Chance isn't just the last name of these rugged
Wyoming cowboys—it's their motto, too!

Read on for a sneak peek at the first title,
SHOULD'VE BEEN A COWBOY

Available June 2011 only from Harlequin® Blaze™.

"THANKS FOR NOT TURNING ON THE LIGHTS," Tyler said. "I'm a mess."

"Not in my book." Even in low light, Alex had a good view of her yellow shirt plastered to her body. It was all he could do not to reach for her, mud and all. But the next move needed to be hers, not his.

She slicked her wet hair back and squeezed some water out of the ends as she glanced upward. "I like the sound of the rain on a tin roof."

"Me, too."

She met his gaze briefly and looked away. "Where's the sink?"

"At the far end, beyond the last stall."

Tyler's running shoes squished as she walked down the aisle between the rows of stalls. She glanced sideways at Alex. "So how much of a cowboy are you these days? Do you ride the range and stuff?"

"I ride." He liked being able to say that. "Why?"

"Just wondered. Last summer, you were still a city boy. You even told me you weren't the cowboy type, but you're…different now."

He wasn't sure if that was a good thing or a bad thing. Maybe she preferred city boys to cowboys. "How am I different?"

"Well, you dress differently, and your hair's a little longer. Your face seems a little more chiseled, but maybe that's because of your hair. Also, there's something else, something harder to define, an attitude…"

"Are you saying I have an attitude?"

"Not in a bad way. It's more like a quiet confidence."

He was flattered, but still he had to laugh. "I just admitted a while ago that I have all kinds of doubts about this event tomorrow. That doesn't seem like quiet confidence to me."

"This isn't about your job, it's about…your…" She took a deep breath. "It's about your sex appeal, okay? I have no business talking about it, because it will only make me want to do things I shouldn't do." She started toward the end of the barn. "Now, where's that sink? We need to get cleaned up and go back to the house. Dinner is probably ready, and I—"

He spun her around and pulled her into his arms, mud and all. "Let's do those things." Then he kissed her, knowing that she would kiss him back, knowing that this time he would take that kiss where he wanted it to go. And she would let him.

Follow Tyler and Alex's wild adventures in
SHOULD'VE BEEN A COWBOY
Available June 2011 only from Harlequin® Blaze™
wherever books are sold.